BASIL THOMSON
THE DARTMOOR ENIGMA

SIR BASIL HOME THOMSON (1861-1939) was educated at Eton and New College Oxford. After spending a year farming in Iowa, he married in 1889 and worked for the Foreign Service. This included a stint working alongside the Prime Minister of Tonga (according to some accounts, he *was* the Prime Minister of Tonga) in the 1890s followed by a return to the Civil Service and a period as Governor of Dartmoor Prison. He was Assistant Commissioner to the Metropolitan Police from 1913 to 1919, after which he moved into Intelligence. He was knighted in 1919 and received other honours from Europe and Japan, but his public career came to an end when he was arrested for committing an act of indecency in Hyde Park in 1925 – an incident much debated and disputed.

His eight crime novels featuring series character Inspector Richardson were written in the 1930's and received great praise from Dorothy L. Sayers among others. He also wrote biographical and criminological works.

Also by Basil Thomson

Richardson's First Case
Richardson Scores Again
The Case of Naomi Clynes
The Case of the Dead Diplomat
Who Killed Stella Pomeroy?
The Milliner's Hat Mystery
A Murder is Arranged

BASIL THOMSON

THE DARTMOOR ENIGMA

With an introduction by
Martin Edwards

DEAN STREET PRESS

Published by Dean Street Press 2016

All Rights Reserved

First published in 1935 by Eldon Press as
Richardson Solves a Dartmoor Mystery

Cover by DSP

Introduction © Martin Edwards 2016

ISBN 978 1 911095 75 0

www.deanstreetpress.co.uk

Introduction

SIR BASIL THOMSON's stranger-than-fiction life was packed so full of incident that one can understand why his work as a crime novelist has been rather overlooked. This was a man whose CV included spells as a colonial administrator, prison governor, intelligence officer, and Assistant Commissioner at Scotland Yard. Among much else, he worked alongside the Prime Minister of Tonga (according to some accounts, he *was* the Prime Minister of Tonga), interrogated Mata Hari and Roger Casement (although not at the same time), and was sensationally convicted of an offence of indecency committed in Hyde Park. More than three-quarters of a century after his death, he deserves to be recognised for the contribution he made to developing the police procedural, a form of detective fiction that has enjoyed lasting popularity.

Basil Home Thomson was born in 1861 – the following year his father became Archbishop of York – and was educated at Eton before going up to New College. He left Oxford after a couple of terms, apparently as a result of suffering depression, and joined the Colonial Service. Assigned to Fiji, he became a stipendiary magistrate before moving to Tonga. Returning to England in 1893, he published *South Sea Yarns*, which is among the 22 books written by him which are listed in Allen J. Hubin's comprehensive bibliography of crime fiction (although in some cases, the criminous content was limited).

Thomson was called to the Bar, but opted to become deputy governor of Liverpool Prison; he later served as governor of such prisons as Dartmoor and Wormwood Scrubs, and acted as secretary to the Prison Commission. In 1913, he became head of C.I.D., which acted as the enforcement arm of British military intelligence after war broke out. When the Dutch exotic dancer and alleged spy Mata Hari arrived in England in 1916, she was arrested and interviewed at length by Thomson at Scotland Yard; she was released, only to be shot the following year by a French firing squad. He gave an account of the interrogation in *Queer People* (1922).

Thomson was knighted, and given the additional responsibility of acting as Director of Intelligence at the Home Office, but in 1921, he was controversially ousted, prompting a heated debate in Parliament: according to *The Times*, "for a few minutes there was pandemonium". The government argued that Thomson was at odds with the Commissioner of the Metropolitan Police, Sir William Horwood (whose own career ended with an ignominious departure fromoffice seven years later), but it seems likely be that covert political machinations lay behind his removal. With many aspects of Thomson's complex life, it is hard to disentangle fiction from fact.

Undaunted, Thomson resumed his writing career, and in 1925, he published *Mr Pepper Investigates*, a collection of humorous short mysteries, the most renowned of which is "The Vanishing of Mrs Fraser". In the same year, he was arrested in Hyde Park for "committing an act in violation of public decency" with a young woman who gave her name as Thelma de Lava. Thomson protested his innocence, but in vain: his trial took place amid a blaze of publicity, and he was fined five pounds. Despite the fact that Thelma de Lava had pleaded guilty (her fine was reportedly paid by a photographer), Thomson launched an appeal, claiming that he was the victim of a conspiracy, but the court would have none of it. Was he framed, or the victim of entrapment? If so, was the reason connected with his past work in intelligence or crime solving? The answers remain uncertain, but Thomson's equivocal responses to the police after being apprehended damaged his credibility.

Public humiliation of this kind would have broken a less formidable man, but Thomson, by now in his mid-sixties, proved astonishingly resilient. A couple of years after his trial, he was appointed to reorganise the Siamese police force, and he continued to produce novels. These included *The Kidnapper* (1933), which Dorothy L. Sayers described in a review for the *Sunday Times* as "not so much a detective story as a sprightly fantasia upon a detective theme." She approved the fact that Thomson wrote "good English very amusingly", and noted that "some of his characters have real charm." Mr Pepper returned in *The Kidnapper*, but in the same year, Thomson introduced his most important character, a Scottish policeman called Richardson.

Thomson took advantage of his inside knowledge to portray a young detective climbing through the ranks at Scotland Yard. And Richardson's rise is amazingly rapid: thanks to the fastest fast-tracking imaginable, he starts out as a police constable, and has become Chief Constable by the time of his seventh appearance – in a book published only four years after the first. We learn little about Richardson's background beyond the fact that he comes of Scottish farming stock, but he is likeable as well as highly efficient, and his sixth case introduces him to his future wife. His inquiries take him – and other colleagues – not only to different parts of England but also across the Channel on more than one occasion: in *The Case of the Dead Diplomat*, all the action takes place in France. There is a zest about the stories, especially when compared with some of the crime novels being produced at around the same time, which is striking, especially given that all of them were written by a man in his seventies.

From the start of the series, Thomson takes care to show the team work necessitated by a criminal investigation. Richardson is a key connecting figure, but the importance of his colleagues' efforts is never minimised in order to highlight his brilliance. In *The Case of the Dead Diplomat*, for instance, it is the trusty

Sergeant Cooper who makes good use of his linguistic skills and flair for impersonation to trap the villains of the piece. Inspector Vincent takes centre stage in *The Milliner's Hat Mystery*, with Richardson confined to the background. He is more prominent in *A Murder is Arranged*, but it is Inspector Dallas who does most of the leg-work.

Such a focus on police team-working is very familiar to present day crime fiction fans, but it was something fresh in the Thirties. Yet Thomson was not the first man with personal experience of police life to write crime fiction: Frank Froest, a legendary detective, made a considerable splash with his first novel, *The Grell Mystery*, published in 1913. Froest, though, was a career cop, schooled in "the university of life" without the benefit of higher education, who sought literary input from a journalist, George Dilnot, whereas Basil Thomson was a fluent and experienced writer whose light, brisk style is ideally suited to detective fiction, with its emphasis on entertainment. Like so many other detective novelists, his interest in "true crime" is occasionally apparent in his fiction, but although *Who Killed Stella Pomeroy?* opens with a murder scenario faintly reminiscent of the legendary Wallace case of 1930, the storyline soon veers off in a quite different direction.

Even before Richardson arrived on the scene, two accomplished detective novelists had created successful police series. Freeman Wills Crofts devised elaborate crimes (often involving ingenious alibis) for Inspector French to solve, and his books highlight the patience and meticulous work of the skilled police investigator. Henry Wade wrote increasingly ambitious novels, often featuring the Oxford-educated Inspector Poole, and exploring the tensions between police colleagues as well as their shared values. Thomson's mysteries are less convoluted than Crofts', and less sophisticated than Wade's, but they make pleasant reading. This is, at least in part, thanks to little touches of detail that are unquestionably authentic – such as senior officers' dread of newspaper criticism, as in *The Dartmoor Enigma*. No other crime writer, after all, has ever had such wide-ranging personal experience of prison management, intelligence work, the hierarchies of Scotland Yard, let alone a desperate personal fight, under the unforgiving glare of the media spotlight, to prove his innocence of a criminal charge sure to stain, if not destroy, his reputation.

Ingenuity was the hallmark of many of the finest detective novels written during "the Golden Age of murder" between the wars, and intricacy of plotting – at least judged by the standards of Agatha Christie, Anthony Berkeley, and John Dickson Carr – was not Thomson's true speciality. That said, *The Milliner's Hat Mystery* is remarkable for having inspired Ian Fleming, while he was working in intelligence during the Second World War, after Thomson's death. In a memo to Rear Admiral John Godfrey, Fleming said: "The following suggestion is used in a book by Basil Thomson: a corpse dressed as an airman, with despatches in his pockets, could be dropped on the coast, supposedly from a parachute that has failed. I understand there is no difficulty in obtaining corpses at the Naval Hospital, but, of course, it would have to be a fresh one." This clever idea became the basis for "Operation Mincemeat", a plan to conceal the invasion of Italy from North Africa.

A further intriguing connection between Thomson and Fleming is that Thomson inscribed copies of at least two of the Richardson books to Kathleen Pettigrew, who was personal assistant to the Director of MI6, Stewart Menzies. She is widely regarded as the woman on whom Fleming based Miss Moneypenny, secretary to James Bond's boss M – the Moneypenny character was originally called "Petty" Petteval. Possibly it was through her that Fleming came across Thomson's book.

Thomson's writing was of sufficiently high calibre to prompt Dorothy L. Sayers to heap praise on Richardson's performance in his third case: "he puts in some of that excellent, sober, straightforward detective work which he so well knows how to do and follows the clue of a post-mark to the heart of a very plausible and proper mystery. I find him a most agreeable companion." The acerbic American critics Jacques Barzun and Wendell Hertig Taylor also had a soft spot for Richardson, saying in *A Catalogue of Crime* that his investigations amount to "early police routine minus the contrived bickering, stomach ulcers, and pub-crawling with which later writers have masked poverty of invention and the dullness of repetitive questioning".

Books in the Richardson series have been out of print and hard to find for decades, and their reappearance at affordable prices is as welcome as it is overdue. Now that Dean Street Press have republished all eight recorded entries in the Richardson case-book, twenty-first century readers are likely to find his company just as agreeable as Sayers did.

Martin Edwards
www.martinedwardsbooks.com

Chapter One

SUPERINTENDENT WITCHARD was checking expense-sheets in his room at Scotland Yard when his clerk looked in.

"Anything fresh this morning?" he asked.

"Nothing out of the ordinary except this letter, sir."

Witchard read the letter carefully and turned to the envelope. "A Devonshire case? Do we know anything about it?"

"No, sir. In ordinary course the Registry would send it down to the Chief Constable of Devon, but I thought you had better see it first."

"Quite right. One can never tell where one of these anonymous letters will land one." He read through the letter again. "Quite a lot of the big cases have come to light first through anonymous letters. I'll let Mr. Morden see it before it goes to the Registry to send off."

Left to himself, the Superintendent read the letter through again.

"Monday

"SIR,

It's my duty to warn you that there's been some funny business over the death of Mr. Dearborn of The Firs, Winterton, the one that had a motor accident up on the moor. The coroner said the cause of the death was the accident. If I was to tell all I know the doctor who gave evidence and the coroner too would look foolish. You ought to stop the burial."

Witchard turned to the envelope, which was addressed to the Chief Constable, Scotland Yard, and bore the postmark, Tavistock. It was of the commonest paper and showed no indication of the maker's name. He carried the letter to Morden's room.

"I thought that you had better see this, sir, before it goes down to the Chief Constable of Devon. So far, it's not a case for us, but it's a curious kind of letter."

Morden read it and handed it back. "Better get it off at once, Mr. Witchard," he said.

But before the letter had time to leave the building the second post from the provinces had reached Scotland Yard and the case began to take shape. The Superintendent of the C.I.D. brought Morden a letter from the Chief Constable of Devon which threw a new light upon the affair.

"SIR (it ran),

"I shall feel much obliged if you will assist me in investigating a case which has arisen in the Winterton Division of this county. This morning my Superintendent brought me the attached anonymous letter, posted in Moorstead.

'Monday

'DEAR SIR,

'I'm writing to you about the death of that Mr. Dearborn of Winterton. Is he going to be buried as if he died as the result of a motor accident like the coroner said? What about a bash on the head with a heavy stick before the accident happened? You bet the murderer's laughing up his sleeve now that he's got away with it.'

"The person referred to is a Mr. Charles Dearborn who lived in a house called The Firs at Winterton. On September 29 he was motoring home across the moor in his Austin Seven car when the car swerved from the centre of the road near the top of Sandiland Hill and partly overturned in the rough ground bordering the road. Dr.

Wilson, the assistant medical officer at the convict prison, who was returning home, stopped his car on seeing the wreckage at the roadside, and finding Mr. Dearborn breathing but unconscious, rendered first aid. He then drove him to Duketon, where he recovered consciousness and was able to give his name and address. Dr. Wilson then drove him home and left him in the hands of his wife, telling her to lose no time in sending for the injured man's own doctor. This, however, Mr. Dearborn would not allow, declaring that he felt better and required no medical attention. Some days passed, and he became so ill that his wife herself sent for the doctor.

"Two days later Mr. Dearborn died. An inquest was held on Monday, 8th; the verdict returned was that death was due to injuries sustained in a motor accident.

"Efforts have been made by my Superintendent to identify the writer of the anonymous letter, but without success.

"I should have attached no importance to an anonymous letter of this kind, but for the fact that one of my officers discovered a broken walking-stick with blood upon it. It was lying among some fern and heather near the top of Sandiland Hill, about four hundred yards from the scene of the motor accident.

"I should be very much obliged if you could spare an experienced detective officer to take charge of the investigation as early as possible. I have arranged for the postponement of the funeral for one or two days, in order to allow time for a detailed surgical examination, in the light of the anonymous letter."

"I thought he was coming to that, Superintendent," observed Morden dryly. "He wants us to take over the case."

"Yes, sir, it's getting a bit thick. We've already got two senior officers working in the provinces and this will make a third."

"Still, we can't refuse. Have we any senior officer with local knowledge?"

The Superintendent considered. "No, sir, but among the juniors there is Sergeant Jago, who was born at Tavistock and passed his early days there. The only chief inspector that could be spared at the moment is Richardson. He's the junior chief inspector, but he's had a varied experience and either by good luck or good management he has got home with his cases."

"Could he start at once?"

"Yes, sir, this afternoon if you like."

"Send him in, then."

In a few moments the junior chief inspector made his appearance. There were those who resented his quick promotion over the heads of officers senior to him, but it was impossible to feel malice towards a man who gave himself no airs, who appeared ever anxious to learn from those junior to himself in rank, and who gave the fullest credit to all who worked under him. It had been his success in a Paris case and the warm recommendation from the Foreign Office that had brought him his last step in promotion.

"You sent for me, sir?" he said to Morden.

"Yes, Mr. Richardson. It was to ask you if you know Dartmoor at all?"

"No, sir. I've been once to the convict prison, but that is all."

"Well, now is your opportunity. The Chief Constable has asked for help in a difficult case which is set out in these papers, and I propose that you take Sergeant Jago with you, as he has an intimate knowledge of the district. Get a copy made of these papers to take with you; get the anonymous letters photographed; get the usual advances and report yourself to the Superintendent at Winterton to-night if you can."

"Very good, sir."

"I don't want you to waste valuable time in writing reports, but if you make any discovery that promises well, you should let us know."

For the next hour Richardson made life a burden to the various departments concerned in sending officers to work in the provinces. But in the end he found himself on the Waterloo platform with his companion in time for the afternoon express to Tavistock. All this had been arranged by telephone from Scotland Yard. The first part of the journey was devoted to a study of the Chief Constable's letter, and to the photographs of the two anonymous letters.

"Have a good look at these photographs, Jago, and tell me what you make of them," said Richardson; "take your time."

Jago studied the envelopes and their postmarks and then scrutinized the text of the letters. "One thing strikes me, Chief Inspector. These two letters were sent off on the same day and the man who posted them could only have posted one in Tavistock and the other in Moorstead if he had a car or motor-lorry."

"Ah! That's where your local knowledge comes in. It's a sound deduction, but why should the owner of the car go to such pains to be anonymous?"

Sergeant Jago shook his head, and Richardson pulled out a map from his pocket. "The distance is only a dozen miles or so, nothing very much for a motor-lorry; but what do motor-lorries carry right across the moor?"

"Mostly granite."

"Oh, then there are granite lorries between Tavistock and Moorstead?"

"Yes, sir, there's Rowe's quarry a mile or two out from Tavistock, where the best granite comes from, and there's a smaller quarry somewhere near Moorstead."

"Have you noticed anything special about the handwriting of these anonymous letters? Would you say that the two were written by the same man?"

Jago studied the photographs again. "Well, if they were, the fellow disguised his hand. The writing in the Commissioner's letter slopes backward much more than the other."

"It does, but that's a familiar trick for a half-educated writer of anonymous letters."

"You think the same man wrote both?"

"I feel sure of it and if I'm right we have something to go upon. First the misspelling. He spells 'burial' with two r's in the Commissioner's letter, and 'buried' in the Chief Constable's also has two r's."

"But I don't see why he should have wanted to appear to be two different people."

"Only because he thought that more notice would be taken of two people than one, and he wanted notice taken, which makes me think that he knows something and that it's not merely a hoax."

"But if he knows something, why shouldn't he come openly to the police and tell them?"

"Ah, that's what we've got to find out. For the moment we're only speculating. Suppose, for instance, that the writer is an ex-convict lately released on licence and that he saw a crime committed; he might think that he wouldn't stand a chance with his bad record if he were accused of committing the crime."

"Yes, I see that, sir."

"At any rate, you with your local knowledge have given us something to work upon—the motor-lorry theory."

They had passed Okehampton and were nearing Tavistock. Richardson packed up his papers and took his modest luggage down from the rack. The train slowed down; a constable in uniform was on the platform; Richardson approached him.

"I'm Chief Inspector Richardson from Scotland Yard."

The constable saluted. "We've been sent to meet you, sir, by Superintendent Carstairs. He had a telegram this afternoon."

"This is Detective Sergeant Jago—a native of Tavistock."

The constable shook hands. "I know your family well, Sergeant," he said.

The drive from Tavistock to Winterton by the main road which skirts the moor was rapidly covered. The car drew up at the police station.

They were met on the steps by Superintendent Carstairs, who shook hands warmly with Richardson.

"I'm very glad you've come down, Chief Inspector. The fact is that with my limited staff I could never have undertaken to solve the case."

"But I shan't be able to get on without you, Superintendent," said Richardson. "It's true that I've brought with me Sergeant Jago, who was born and brought up in Tavistock and has knowledge of the locality, but naturally he has no acquaintance with the dead man's affairs and you would have."

"That is the trouble, Chief Inspector. No one knows anything of the late Mr. Dearborn's affairs—not even his wife. What I propose to do for you is this. I'll show you the broken stick which was picked up by one of my officers about a quarter of a mile from the scene of the accident, and then, tomorrow morning I propose to introduce you to the widow and let you question her in any way you please. I want you to remember that whenever you require transport the police car will be at your service. In fact, I am turning over the case to you entirely."

"The body has not been buried yet?"

"No. Dr. Symon, who was called in by the widow to attend the deceased just before he died, is a young man without very much experience, and the verdict at the inquest was given on his evidence. You will probably desire to have a second medical opinion in view of the finding of the broken stick and the anonymous letter written to me."

"That was not the only one, Superintendent. The Commissioner in London also received one in the same handwriting. I have brought photographs of the two letters for you to see. Now may I have a look at the broken stick?"

"Step into my office, Mr. Richardson. We can dispose of all these questions now." He led the way to a little room, scrupulously tidy, and called for his clerk. "See that we're not disturbed, Henry."

"Very good, sir."

"Now sit down, Mr. Richardson, and make yourself at home. This office will always be at your disposal."

He took a bunch of keys from his pocket, unlocked a drawer and took from it the top of a heavy walking-stick with a silver band. "You will see the bloodstains on the crook."

"With a hair adhering to it," observed Richardson. "I suppose the bloodstains have not yet been examined to see whether it's human blood, nor the hair compared with that of the dead man?"

The Superintendent chuckled in his beard.

"No, down here I'm afraid we don't work at such high pressure. The fact is that when the Chief Constable told me on the telephone that you were coming, I thought it better not to interfere with any possible evidence."

"Have you any doctor in your mind, say from Plymouth, who could make a second examination of the body with Dr. Symon?"

"Well, yes; I thought of calling in Dr. Fraser. He's a man of about forty-five, well known to the local magistrates, and very cautious when giving an opinion. If you approve I can telephone to him this evening to be up here to-morrow morning."

"Very well, and now I'll show you the photographs of the letters."

Richardson laid the two photographs on the desk. Superintendent Carstairs took out a pair of glasses, polished them with his handkerchief and bent over the letters, breathing hard. It was clear that he was more at home in dealing with his staff in out-door-work than in comparing documents. Richardson felt, more than saw, that he was waiting for a lead. It was a pathetic spectacle—this weather-beaten, bearded superintendent, who more than filled his office chair, bending over documents on which he knew that he could give no useful opinion. Richardson came to his rescue.

"You see, Mr. Carstairs, that the letters were written by the same hand and that the writer tried to disguise his handwriting by tilting the characters backward in the letter to the Commissioner. But the misspelling is the same in each."

The Superintendent nodded.

"Then, if you look at the postmarks you can see that they were posted in places a good many miles apart. The writer, therefore, must have been in possession of a car or motor-lorry."

Superintendent Carstairs acquiesced and handed back the photographs, glad to be rid of them. "Now, Mr. Richardson, you must be tired after your journey. I've found quarters for you and your sergeant at the local hotel—the Duchy Arms. If you will come round here at nine-thirty to-morrow morning I will introduce you to Mrs. Dearborn."

Chapter Two

OCTOBER 11 was one of those rarely warm and beautiful days that seem to be sent to leave dwellers on the moor with a memory of the dead summer when the pall of mist and rain is due to descend upon them.

At half-past nine the Superintendent looked in to say that it was not too early to take Richardson over to Mrs. Dearborn. "I telephoned to her this morning, telling her to expect you, so you will find her prepared. Dr. Fraser will be at the house for the medical examination of the body at half-past eleven. Probably you will want to see him."

"What about Sergeant Jago, Mr. Carstairs? Will the lady be prepared to receive two of us?"

"If you take my advice, Chief Inspector, you will see her alone. She isn't an excitable person, but I fancy that she will be more communicative if you are by yourself. While you are talking to her, Sergeant Jago might be looking over the car, which is in the private garage at The Firs."

Mrs. Dearborn opened the door to them in person. She was a thin, worn woman, who looked older than her age; there was an air of faded gentility about her. She was dressed in black. "This is the gentleman of whom I spoke to you on the telephone," said Carstairs. "Chief Inspector Richardson of Scotland Yard."

Richardson shook hands with her and noticed that her fingers were rough like those of one accustomed to domestic work.

"Will you come into the sitting-room, Mr. Richardson?" she said; "we shall be quite quiet there. And you, Mr. Carstairs?"

"No, I've my work to do. But I hope you will tell Mr. Richardson everything you know and keep nothing back. While he is here I should like his assistant to have a look at the car in the garage. May I have the key please?"

She took a key from a hook in the hall and gave it to him. "No one has touched the car since it was brought in."

After a sympathetic reference to her loss, Richardson began his questioning. "I think I ought to ask you first, how long you have been married to Mr. Dearborn?"

"We were married in Plymouth a year ago, but I had been keeping house for him for two years before that. You see, when my father died, his pension died with him and I was left very badly off. I saw an advertisement in a Plymouth newspaper, for a housekeeper, and I answered it. Mr. Dearborn invited me to an interview and that was how I first met him."

"Until you answered that advertisement you knew nothing of your husband?"

"No; I had never heard of him in my life."

"Had he been living long in Winterton?"

"No, he told me he had only just bought this house."

"Did he say who the house agent was who sold it to him?"

"No."

"Nor from what part of the country he came? Because I gather that he was not a Plymouth man."

"No. It may seem strange to you, but he told me nothing of his past life and I asked him no questions, because I thought that he would tell me of his own accord if he wanted to."

"So you never knew anything about his former profession?"

"No, nothing."

"Nor about his friends and relations?"

"No; he told me he had no near relations, and apart from business letters from tradesmen, he received no correspondence by post."

"What was his age?"

"There I can answer you. At the time of our marriage he gave it as thirty-eight."

"He had a bank in Plymouth, I suppose?"

"Yes. It was the Union Bank—because when he showed me his will, I saw that the manager of the Union Bank was his sole executor and he explained that he had left everything he possessed to me."

"What did he do with his time?"

"Well, he was a great newspaper reader, and that took up the greater part of his mornings. Lately he has had the quarry to visit, but before he bought that he used to take long walks."

"By himself?"

"Yes, always by himself. When he first came people used to call on him, but he never returned their visits nor answered their invitations to tennis-parties and the like, so I suppose they grew tired of asking him."

"And they haven't renewed their invitations since your marriage?"

"No, but I have always plenty to occupy me at home, looking after the house and garden."

"You have a maidservant?"

"Yes, a Devonshire girl who has been with us ever since I came to the house."

"Have you a gardener?"

She smiled. "You are talking to the gardener at this moment. Sometimes I have to get in a jobbing gardener to do the digging, but otherwise I look after the garden myself."

"How long has your husband had a car?"

"He bought it about six months ago. It was like a new toy to him. Two or three times a week, except in very bad weather, he would go for long drives over the moor. I suppose he wasn't a very experienced driver and that that was the cause of the accident."

"He was conscious between the time of his accident and his death a week later?"

"Oh, yes; certainly on the first two days after the accident."

"And he never told you how it happened?"

"Yes; he said that his foot-brake didn't work, but my impression was that he had his foot on the wrong lever and mistook the accelerator for the brake."

"Did he speak of having met anyone shortly before the mishap?"

"No. As I told you, he did not know any of his neighbours."

"So it comes to this—that neither you nor he were on speaking terms with anyone in Winterton?"

"He was not, but I have one friend in the place—a young naval officer, Lieutenant Cosway, whose parents live in the second house from this, in that direction"—she pointed towards Plymouth. "You see, I have a Siamese kitten. One day Mr. Cosway was passing with his dog and it chased my kitten up a tree. He called off the dog and apologized, but the kitten was afraid to come down and so he took off his coat and climbed the tree. I got frightened because the higher he climbed the higher went the kitten, and I was afraid that the tree, which was bending with his weight, would break and both of them would be killed. However, he rescued the little beast and brought it down in his arms.

"Since then he has been in to look at my garden once or twice. You see, he has a dockyard appointment at Devonport and often comes up to Winterton to see his family."

"Did he never make your husband's acquaintance?"

"No, my husband always happened to be out when he came."

"Then if your husband had no friends in Winterton, at any rate he had no enemies?"

She appeared startled. "Enemies? Why do you ask that?"

Up to this point her manner had been so colourless and her replies so composed that Richardson had scarcely realized that he was dealing with a woman of flesh and blood. She left him in no doubt on that point now.

"The questions you have been asking me are surely very unusual. Do you always cross-examine people on their private lives like this in the case of an accident? I think that I am entitled to some explanation."

"You are quite right, Mrs. Dearborn. I ought to have explained sooner why I have been asking these questions. Someone has been writing anonymous letters to the police, suggesting that your husband's death was due, not to the motor accident alone, but to an attack made upon him by someone on the road, and in order to clear this up there is to be another medical examination this morning."

"But this is ridiculous. My husband was fully conscious after his accident, and I am sure he would have told me if he had been attacked."

"Well, we can only wait for the result of the medical examination, and until that is made there is nothing for you to worry about. You see, Mrs. Dearborn, anonymous letters in most cases turn out to be malicious and ill-informed, but it is unwise entirely to ignore them as I think you will agree."

"I quite see that, and now that I know the reason for your questions I will answer them all to the best of my ability. The only point on which I can give you but little help is on my husband's affairs, because he never took me into his confidence."

"Thank you, Mrs. Dearborn. I won't worry you with any more questions now."

Richardson went round to the garage where he found Sergeant Jago with evidence on his clothes and hands of having made an exhaustive survey of the car. Before joining the Metropolitan Police Jago had worked in a Tavistock garage and the experience had been useful to him; indeed there had been a time when the Public Carriage Department at Scotland Yard had competed with the C.I.D. for his services.

"Well, young man," said Richardson, "what discoveries have you made?"

"The engine's all right, but the steering-gear is badly messed up. There's nothing whatever wrong with the brakes; they couldn't have contributed to the accident, but there's one funny thing. These cars are always furnished with a starting-handle in case the batteries run down, and there's not one in the car or anywhere in the garage. The speedometer marks a run of sixteen miles, which would mean that the car had been about as far as Moorstead on the day of the accident."

"I should like to take advantage of this fine day by running out to the scene of the accident. You had better come with me and we'll get the Superintendent to give us the man who found that broken walking-stick. Come along with me to the police station."

They found Superintendent Carstairs in his little office. "Certainly you can have the car, and as it happens the man who will drive you is the very man who found the broken stick." He rang a bell and the car was brought round.

"My God! What a road!" exclaimed Richardson, as they negotiated the hill leading up from Sandiland. "It's like the side of a house." But the car took the hill on her second speed, and before they came to the top she pulled up well to the side of the track. The driver jumped down.

"This is where we found the car, sir. It had turned nearly over. You can see the wheel marks there in that broken heather."

"And where did you find the broken stick?"

"If you'll come up the hill a little way, sir, I'll show you. It was me that found it."

He led the way up in the direction of Duketon and stopped at a point where the hill was a little less steep. The heather was particularly tall and dense at this point.

"I marked the place with three little stones, sir. Here they are, and there's the place where the broken stick was lying."

Richardson cast an eye round. The surface of the road was rough at this point; the traffic to and from Duketon and the downpours of rain had washed gutters in the surface.

"It's almost useless to attempt to keep a tarred road in good order with all the summer traffic of char-à-bancs and lorries. The rain comes down here like a water-course."

"What I want to look for," said Richardson, "is the other half of the broken stick and the starting-handle of the Austin Seven. They must both be somewhere about."

The three men began to quarter the ground systematically, beginning on the near side of the road. Richardson was the first to exclaim. He stooped and held up a starting-handle already coated with rust but not pitted with it. Sergeant Jago came over to him and identified his find as belonging to an Austin Seven. It was now the turn of the driver. "Here we are," he cried, "if this isn't the other half of the stick I'm a Dutchman."

"It certainly looks like the same wood," said Richardson; "but we'll have to fit the two pieces together before we can be sure. What's your theory about what happened?" he asked the driver, with the ghost of a smile playing about his mouth.

"The way I figure it out is this, sir. Mr. Dearborn wasn't an experienced driver. He let his engine stop, and then, not liking to go down the hill without it, he got out with the starting-handle to swing the engine. While he was stooping to fit it in a man came up behind him and whacked him over the head with that stick."

"What was the motive?"

"Highway robbery, sir. There's quite a lot of quarrymen out of work in the autumn, and it was a temptation to one of them to knock the gentleman down and go through his pockets. Then he threw away the broken stick and starting-handle into the heather and got away with his find. You see, it's a very lonely road."

"But why did Dearborn not tell the police as soon as the doctor had driven him down to Winterton?"

"Loss of memory, sir. After a whack on the head like that, a man remembers nothing of what's just happened to him. It's true that he managed to start the car again and to drive on, but a man in that state in a car was asking for trouble. And then all he would remember afterwards would be the accident."

"I see," said Richardson dryly. "What's your theory, Sergeant Jago?"

Jago knew his chief in this mood and was not disposed to commit himself. "I would rather wait until we've gone further into the case before expressing an opinion," he said.

"Wise man; you'll go far in your profession," observed Richardson. He did not commit himself, either, to any theory of his own. He turned to the driver. "You'll have a job to turn your car in this narrow road. What's wrong with running on into Duketon and letting me have a look at the village?"

"Right, sir, and while we're about it we might run on to the prison gate because that's where the doctor took the deceased when he picked him up after the accident. It's no distance."

Half a mile farther up the hill brought them to the village.

"Pull up here," called Richardson when they reached the branching of two roads and the car had turned to the left. "Where does that other road take you to?"

"Bridgend and on to Moorstead."

"And this one?"

"To the prison and on to Tavistock."

"And which road was Dearborn taking?"

"He was coming from Moorstead. We know that from people who saw him pass."

"Right. Then go ahead towards the prison."

They passed the granite church built by the French war prisoners of Napoleonic times; passed cottages made hideous by walls tarred to keep out the winter damp, and reached the prison gate, on which the old motto, *Parcere subjectis* (Spare the Conquered), was still legible. On either side of the gate were the houses of the superior officers, and the gate itself was a double one with the guard-room of the armed civil guard between.

"I should like to have a word with the medical officer who picked up the deceased. You might see whether he can be found."

The driver went to the inner gate and called the gatekeeper, to whom he explained that two officers from Scotland Yard would like to speak to Dr. Wilson, the assistant medical officer, if he could be got hold of.

"He'll be here in less than a minute," said the gatekeeper, glancing at the clock in the lodge. "He's just finishing his round in the hospital and will be coming out to lunch."

Indeed, it was a procession of prison officers that now crowded at the inner gate, for the convicts had all been locked up for the dinner-hour and the warders were giving up their keys. The routine of this ceremony was the result of more than fifty years of accidents and mistakes and it went like clockwork. Each principal warder handed over his bunch of cell keys with the words, "All correct." The gatekeeper cast a wary eye over each bunch to see that no key was missing, and let the warders go their several ways. Suddenly the group about the gate opened a lane to allow a young man in plain clothes to take precedence.

"Here comes the assistant surgeon," said the gatekeeper, turning round. He took the hospital keys and murmured to Dr. Wilson that two police officers from London were waiting outside to speak to him.

"What's it all about?" asked the young doctor.

"They didn't tell me that, sir. You'll find them in that car."

As Dr. Wilson approached the car, Richardson jumped down and introduced himself. "We've come down to inquire about the man whom you picked up a fortnight ago after a motor accident."

"Ah, yes, you mean Mr. Dearborn of Winterton?"

"You know he is dead, sir?"

"Yes," said the doctor. "I saw the account of the inquest in the papers; the death was due to the accident."

"I understand that Dr. Symon who attended him testified that the cause of death was an injury sustained in a motor accident. I wanted to ask you, sir, whether possibly there may have been another cause of death."

"He had had a knock on the head, certainly—a nasty blow which had cut the scalp and it was bleeding a good deal, but he recovered consciousness while I was dressing the wound, and I assumed that when his car turned over his head had come into violent contact with the frame of the car. In that case Dr. Symon's evidence as to the cause of death would be correct."

"How was the car lying when you found it?"

"Well, it was half turned over, that is to say, two of the wheels were in the air. Dearborn was lying with his head against the inside of the body. I assumed that the wound on the top of the head was the result of a sharp impact against the woodwork of the roof, which, of course, is covered with lining material, but not so thick as to protect the head of a person thrown violently against it."

Richardson told him about the anonymous letters, asking him to treat the information as confidential.

"You see, sir, it might be fatal to my inquiries if this got into the press. Another medical examination is to be made."

"Who is making it?"

"Dr. Fraser from Plymouth."

"You couldn't have chosen a better man."

Chapter Three

When the car drew up at Mrs. Dearborn's door, the two doctors were just coming out. Richardson jumped down and presented himself as a Chief Inspector from Scotland Yard. Dr. Fraser was a grave, grey man of between forty and fifty.

"I don't wish to intrude upon your conversation, gentlemen," said Richardson, "but before you go and before you make your report I must ask you to see the damaged car in the garage, in order to determine whether the injuries on the deceased's head could have been produced by impact with the car roof at the time of the accident. I ask this because I have just come from the scene of the accident, where we have made one or two small discoveries."

Dr. Fraser looked at him sombrely, as if he resented interference by a layman. Richardson turned to Jago. "Go and get the key of the garage, and lead the way."

"We were going to inspect the car in any case, Chief Inspector, but this is purely a surgical matter."

"I am quite aware of that, Dr. Fraser. My only wish was to give you all the material for your finding. For example, here is what we believe to be the missing half of the broken stick shown to you by Superintendent Carstairs."

Dr. Fraser took the stick, weighed it in his hand and passed it to Dr. Symon.

"We have also found the starting-handle of Mr. Dearborn's car. It had been thrown some ten yards into the heather."

"We are not detective officers," said Dr. Fraser. "Our task is to determine only the cause of death, and this we are both prepared to do. The steps to be taken in consequence of our report are not for us to decide. The facts that we are prepared to report are that the deceased had an abnormally thin skull; that he died from hæmorrhage of the brain in consequence of a blow from some blunt instrument which shattered the skull at the point of impact. Whether this was a blow received from the roof of the car when it turned over, or from some outside agency such as that broken stick, is rather a matter for you than for us, but as you seem to desire it, we will examine the car carefully and tell you our opinion." With these words Dr. Fraser followed Jago into the garage and climbed into the little Austin Seven. He felt and examined the roofing and then called to Dr. Symon to climb up beside him.

Richardson did not hear their conversation, but he saw them paying particular attention to a spot in the roof immediately behind the driving seat. It was stained with blood which had dried. Presently they got out again and Dr. Fraser spoke.

"Where did you find this broken stick?" he asked.

"A few yards from the spot where we found the starting-handle. It was two hundred and seventy-one paces from the place where the car overturned. I paced the distance myself."

"Do you suggest, then, that the deceased was assaulted from behind with that stick while he was sitting in the car?"

"At this stage I suggest nothing, doctor," said Richardson; "but we have to account for the stick and the starting-handle being that distance from the place where the car overturned with the deceased in it. It is for you to say whether a man who had sustained a fracture of the skull could have set his car in motion and driven nearly three hundred yards before running into a ditch."

Dr. Fraser drew Dr. Symon aside and began to talk to him in a low tone. Fraser appeared to be urging some course of action upon Symon. He gained acquiescence and turned again to Richardson. "In view of what you have told us, my colleague is prepared to admit that the evidence he gave at the inquest may have been a little over positive, but we must bear in mind that the deceased was conscious, and had said nothing about any attack being made upon him."

"I quite see Dr. Symon's point of view, but I presume that the coroner will not hold a second inquest."

"No, because the police will do all that is necessary in the interests of justice. I shall see the coroner and explain the circumstances to him."

"You have solved my difficulties entirely, Dr. Fraser. I presume that you have got all the necessary materials for your report and that the funeral can now take place."

"That is so. Our report will go to the Superintendent of police here."

Without another word the two doctors went towards their car. Sergeant Jago gazed at their retreating backs with disapproval. "They seem to think that we are causing a lot of unnecessary trouble for nothing."

"Doctors like to be regarded by laymen as infallible and incapable of making mistakes. This weakness is not altogether unknown among detective officers. You are young in the service, Sergeant Jago; you should bear this in mind. And now to lunch."

After a hasty meal, Richardson and Jago got the police car to drive them to the Union Bank in Plymouth. It was an unfortunate hour for both the manager and the cashier were away at lunch and the two junior clerks and bank messenger were the only representatives of the staff. From one of these Richardson ascertained that the late Mr. Dearborn had an account there.

"I will call in again a little after two o'clock if you will kindly ask the manager to keep that time clear for me."

"You ought to see the Hoe now you're here, sir, and have a few minutes to spare," observed Jago. "I can show you the place where Sir Francis Drake was playing bowls when the Spanish Armada was sighted." He led his chief uphill to the famous Hoe and pointed out the spot identified by the local historians. It was a perfect day. Over Drake's Island one could see an expanse of calm sea stretching towards the Eddystone lighthouse. They walked up and down the almost deserted promenade; the good folk of Plymouth were enjoying their midday meal.

Richardson looked at his watch. "It's now one minute to two. Let's go down to the bank and see whether the manager is a punctual person."

The messenger intimated that Mr. Todd, the manager, was expecting them. He ushered them into a little room on the left of the entrance, where an energetic-looking little man received them. Richardson tendered his official card and introduced Sergeant Jago as his assistant.

"I have come to ask you a few questions about the late Mr. Dearborn of Winterton, who, I understand, was a customer of this bank."

"He was, and as I am his sole executor, I ought really to be attending his funeral this afternoon."

"I can relieve your mind on that score, Mr. Todd. The funeral has had to be postponed for a day or two. Probably it will take place to-morrow, but in any case I will send you a telephone message."

The manager looked startled. "Postponed? Oh, I see!" He picked up Richardson's card. "Something has transpired since the coroner's inquest and you have come down from London to investigate. Does it mean that foul play is suspected?"

"I presume that anything I say will be treated by you as strictly confidential. Some anonymous letters have reached the police, alleging that the motor accident was not the cause of death, and in consequence of a request from the Chief Constable I have been sent down to carry out inquiries. Mrs. Dearborn told me that her husband was a customer of your bank and I am anxious to put a few questions to you about his account."

"Certainly. I shall be glad to answer anything you want to ask."

"My first question is, when and under what circumstances did Mr. Dearborn open an account with you?"

"I can give you the exact date. It was about three years ago, and the account was opened in the simplest possible way. Mr. Dearborn walked into the bank one afternoon and asked to see me. He told me that he had just disposed of a block of real property in London by private sale and had brought the proceeds with him in cash. I suppose I looked surprised, because he went on to say that he had insisted upon a cash payment and that the purchaser had met him by sending to his bank for the money in notes. The amount was twenty-five thousand pounds. He picked up a little handbag and took out a bundle of notes of large denomination and asked me to count them. It was, as you may imagine, a very unusual transaction, and I put down my new customer as a person of eccentric habits."

"Did he say whether he was a Londoner? Or in subsequent conversations did he ever give you a hint as to where he had come from?"

"Now you speak of it I can't remember that he did. I never questioned that he was a Londoner after hearing from him that he had been the owner of house property there."

"I suppose that during the last three years you became fairly intimate?"

"Intimate is scarcely the word. I've never been to his house if that's what you mean. I know that he's married, but I've never been introduced to his wife. On the other hand, I consented to become executor to his will as a matter of business."

"What did he do with his money? Invest it, leave it on deposit, or what?"

"He frequently asked my advice about investments, since two per cent, was all that I could give him on deposit. A few months ago a quarry near Moorstead was for sale. It had banked with us and we knew that it could be made a paying concern. I brought it to his notice and he went over to inspect it and finally bought it. Since then I'm told that he made regular visits in a little car that he had acquired—I suppose the same car in which he was driving at the time of the accident."

"I understand that he has left everything by will to his widow. Do you know who drew the will?"

"He told me that he had drafted it himself. At any rate the legal terminology seemed to be all right."

"Had he actually paid for the quarry?"

"Yes; there was some question about turning it into a limited company with himself as chairman, but he wouldn't hear of it. If he touched it at all, he kept saying, he must buy it outright, and as the price was low, I did nothing to dissuade him."

"How much did he pay for it?"

"Seven thousand pounds." "Which left about eighteen thousand on deposit with you?"

"Yes. I can give you the exact figures if you wait till to-morrow."

"Do you know what he did when he went out to the quarry?"

"No. He told me once that he went through the books and orders with the foreman."

"You do not know whether he had occasion to sack any of the hands? Because these discharged men are sometimes vindictive if they fail to get another job."

"I believe he told me that he had been obliged to discharge one man because he was making the others discontented. I think the man was a communist and had had a row with the foreman, a staunch conservative. It seemed to me a rather inadequate reason for getting rid of a man."

"Do you remember the man's name?"

"No, I don't, but he was one of those half-baked political agitators that one finds almost everywhere."

"I've one more question to ask, Mr. Todd. The motor accident took place on the 29th of September. Did Mr. Dearborn cash a cheque on that or the previous day? I suppose he had to cash cheques regularly to pay the wages at the quarry. What I want to get at is whether he was carrying any larger sum than usual on that day."

"If you'll wait here, I'll examine his account."

In two minutes the manager was back.

"I find that on September 29 he drew out the same amount, almost to a penny, that he had drawn every Friday since he had the quarry. Saturday was his pay-day; the accident took place on his return journey, and therefore the presumption is that he had very little money in his pockets."

"That seems to dispose of the theory that he was waylaid by a highway robber. Thank you, Mr. Todd. Perhaps you'll let me see you again if any other point arises. I think I will run out to the quarry this afternoon."

The driver of the police car seemed to know the road to the Moorstead quarry well. He covered the distance at breakneck speed. Richardson and Jago alighted and went through the quarry gate as if the place belonged to them. The quarry was cut out of the hillside; the cliff exposed by the quarrying operations was of a light rose colour.

Jago looked round him critically. "They've let their spoil-heap encroach; it'll soon be over the road if they don't look out. That's always the way with quarries that are full of orders."

Richardson's attention was fixed on a thick-set little man who was jumping and sliding down the quarry face and making his way towards them. This was John Lawrence, the quarry foreman, who had mistaken them for customers come to order granite. His face fell when Richardson introduced himself.

"Police officers from London, are you? Well then, just step into my office. If the men know who you are there'll be no getting any work out of them for the rest of the day." He was careful to leave the door of the office open to guard against eavesdroppers. "Office" was a strange name to use for the little cubby-hole in which the three men found themselves. A charcoal stove poisoned the atmosphere; a sloping desk, made by hands more inured to dressing granite than to carpentering, filled more than a quarter of the available space. There were two stools in the hut, but only two; Jago had to stand.

"You want to know whether Mr. Dearborn seemed well the last day he came to the quarry. As far as I could see he was in his usual health. He went through the books and orders; he insisted on going out to see the men at work; he handed over to me their weekly wages to be paid. No, there was nothing wrong with him that day. He drove off at his usual time—a little after four—and that was the last time I saw him. I suppose his executors are in charge of the quarry now and will sell it to someone who knows nothing about quarrying."

"Do you have any trouble with the men?"

"No, the men are all right, if people will only leave them alone."

"Do you mean that they have agitators among them?"

"They had one, but Mr. Dearborn soon gave him the push when I told him what was going on."

"Who was that?"

"A fellow named Dick Pengelly, a Cornishman and a blighter if ever there was one."

"Does he come up worrying the men now?"

"Not now. He used to come up at knocking-off time and tell the men they ought to go on strike because Mr, Dearborn had fired him without any reason. I told Mr. Dearborn about this the day before his accident, and as he was going out of the quarry he saw Pengelly hanging about, and I tell you he gave him a proper dressing-down—talked of going down to the police about him. I believe that he frightened him out of his boots—at any rate I've never seen him up here since, and one of the men told me that he's left the district and gone off to get work somewhere else. I'll say one thing for him—he was a good quarry-smith."

"A smith? Do you mean a blacksmith?"

"Why, yes, I suppose you'd call him a blacksmith. He's the man who welds the points on to the jumpers and tempers them. I tell you I had a job to replace Pengelly. It needs good judgment to point and temper a jumper."

Richardson put both hands to his forehead. "I don't even know what a jumper is," he confessed.

"Well then, you'd better come out with me and I'll show you."

The foreman liked nothing better than to expatiate on his trade. He took them first to a blacksmith's shop, where Pengelly's successor was welding new points to broken jumpers; showed his two visitors the essential tool in granite-quarrying—the jumper, a long crowbar with a huge bulb of metal in the middle of it to give the weight necessary to pierce the hardest granite; took them up to the quarry face where two men were drilling holes.

"You see, these holes have to be four or five inches deep, and you see this little tool," taking up a spatula of iron used for lifting the granite dust out of the holes; "now these men have got to drive twelve holes into this granite before we put in the points and feathers."

"Points and feathers?"

"Yes, these are the feathers. The smith cuts them out of old spades and shovels." He took up two thin slivers of steel. "These are the feathers and this is a point." He exhibited a steel point slightly larger than the hole made by the jumper. "When the twelve holes are made three inches apart and the points and feathers are adjusted, one of these men goes along with a sledge-hammer and drives in the points one after another. They ring almost like a bell for the first few taps and then there's a dull sound and you know that the whole block has been detached from the quarry face. Then all we have to do is stick in wedges and roll the block down on to that spoil-heap below, where it falls soft. That's quarrying and it's highly skilled labour, I can tell you, because you've got to study the grain of the granite and make sure that there are no fissures ahead of you. You know, of course, that there's copper and tin to be found in the fissures of the granite—the one running south-west and the other north-east—but we don't find any hereabouts."

As they were returning to the office and were out of hearing of the men, Richardson asked, "Where would Pengelly be likely to go to get another job as a quarry-smith?"

"Ah! There you're asking me something. He might try Rowe's Quarry this side of Tavistock, or go off into Cornwall where there are several quarries about, but my men say that he never let anyone know where he was going."

"Where did he live when working here?"

"In lodgings in Moorstead; he'd no family."

"Do you know the address?"

"Yes, I have it in my book." He looked through a well-thumbed note-book and gave it. "Mrs. Duke, Sun Lane, Moorstead."

Richardson noted this down, shook hands with the foreman, and told him that he had learned more about granite-quarrying than he could ever have found in books.

Chapter Four

THE TWO DETECTIVE officers made for the police car.

"We haven't wasted our time," said Jago as he went.

"I suppose now you'll have a talk to this Mrs. Duke in Moorstead?"

"You think that everything points to Pengelly being the murderer?" inquired Richardson.

"Yes, sir, except for one thing. I should have expected him to have used a crowbar instead of a walking-stick, but I suppose you'll go into that when you see the woman at his lodgings."

"We shall have a lot to go into when we see the woman at his lodgings," said Richardson thoughtfully.

They got into the car and gave the address in Sun Lane, Moorstead.

The driver looked doubtful. "I'll have to ask the way when we get to the town," he said. "I've never heard of Sun Lane myself."

Moorstead was typical of a moorland town. It lay below the level of the moor itself, and what had once been bogland and heather was now under cultivation. For the rest it might have been centuries old, for the whole town was built of granite, the door-posts and lintels of the older houses made of roughly squared stone with the jumper holes still showing; brick had only lately invaded the main street.

The car pulled up before a public-house, where the driver asked for Sun Lane. It appeared that this was down the second street on the right and the first on the left. "But you won't be able to get down it with that car, mister; it's narrow and there's no way out at the end, nor any way to turn a car as long as yours."

So the car pulled up at the end of Sun Lane, which was little more than an alley, very imperfectly kept and cleaned. There were no pavements and the denizens of the lane seemed to be prone to empty their slops before their doors.

Tousled heads protruded from every window as the officers picked their way along the lane. A woman with a broom in her hand was sweeping her paved kitchen, which appeared to serve also as a chicken-run. To Richardson's inquiry for the house of Mrs. Duke she had a ready answer. "Mrs. Duke, you're wanted!" she bawled across the street, and a grizzled head that sorely needed the attention of a comb appeared in a doorway. "There you are; that's Mrs. Duke herself," said the woman.

The lady in question stripped off her apron and smoothed down the front of her skirt in honour of obviously distinguished visitors. The officers crossed the road and Richardson opened the conversation by asking whether she had once had a lodger called Richard Pengelly. It did not escape him that there was a certain stiffening in her manner as she replied in the affirmative.

"He's not here now?" asked Richardson.

"No, he's left the district some days ago."

"Can you tell me where I can find him?"

"I'd tell you fast enough if I knew, but he just went off—to look for work, he said."

"How did he go—by motor-coach or rail?"

"I can't tell you that, sir." A gleam of curiosity shot from her eyes. "What did you want to see him about?" she asked. "Perhaps I can help you."

"Nothing much, madam. It was only to ask him a few questions."

"Perhaps my daughter Susie might know where he went to. I'll fetch her if you'll sit down."

Apparently the premises were of some size. Richardson had noticed that there was a gate wide enough to admit a car, and that it led into a yard in which there were the marks of rubber tyres. So the Duke family possessed a motor vehicle of some kind.

Jago was about to speak, but Richardson held up his hand. He had heard Mrs. Duke approaching with her daughter, and his sharp ears had caught the words uttered in an undertone, "It's my belief that they're police, so be careful what you say."

Susie Duke was a self-possessed young person with sharp features. She presented herself for questioning with perfect composure and replied to the inquiry as to what had become of their late lodger with almost redundant explanations. "It was this way, sir. I don't rightly know whether Mr. Pengelly was turned out of his job at the quarry properly or not. He said it was only because he gave a back-answer to his boss. It was nothing to do with his work. Anyway, he had to go and find another job, and that wasn't easy because you see each quarry has its own smith and they seldom change him. By this time he may be miles away over in Cornwall."

"How did he go?"

"Oh, well, when a man's looking for work in these parts he tramps it; it makes it easier for him when it comes to seeing the foreman and asking him for a job."

"I see you have a car here," said Richardson indifferently.

"Oh, you mean my brother's baby lorry. Yes, he uses it for carrying vegetables and light loads like that, but it isn't here now. It wanted something doing to it and so it's at Tavistock being repaired."

"Is your brother in Tavistock?"

"No, he's on the sick-list upstairs; it was lucky he was well enough to take it into Tavistock before he fell sick."

"Is he well enough to talk to us if we go upstairs?"

"Oh, you mustn't do that. The doctor wouldn't like it; you might catch it; he's got the 'flu."

Sergeant Jago put in a word here. "Do you know which garage your brother goes to in Tavistock? Is it Quilter's?"

"I'm sure I can't tell you. He'd know, of course, but he's asleep just now and it wouldn't do to wake him. But it's Mr. Pengelly you're looking for, isn't it? Not my brother?"

"That's right. Well, I can't say that you've been very helpful to us, Miss Duke, but perhaps you'll remember more when we come to see you again. You'll say good-bye to your mother for us, won't you?"

And when they were out of earshot of Sun Lane, Jago delivered himself of the comment, "I don't know what you think about that young female, Mr. Richardson, but I don't believe a word of what she's told us."

"Nor I. I suppose that you thought I let her off rather lightly with my questions, but I don't want to see her again until I've got some information about her from other sources. With a young woman of that type you must have some facts up your sleeve if you want to keep her in the straight and narrow path. It will be easy to get at the truth when once we find that small lorry that her brother drives. It's late now for going round the garages in Tavistock; we'll have to put it off until to-morrow morning."

Superintendent Carstairs came out to them when he heard the sound of the car. "You seem to have had a busy day, Chief Inspector."

"Yes, Mr. Carstairs; thanks to you for lending me your car, we have. We've seen Dearborn's bank manager and found out from him that the deceased man had lately bought a quarry near Moorstead."

"Why, that must be what they call the Red Quarry. I didn't know that it had changed hands. Had he been out there on the day of his accident?"

"He had. We've been out there this afternoon and had a talk with the foreman, and now we want to get hold of a man named Richard Pengelly, who was dismissed by Dearborn and may have a grudge against him. He was the quarry-smith. That's not all we did. We went to the place where he lodged and were filled up with tales by his landlady's daughter, and so to-morrow, if you'll lend us your car again, we propose to go to Tavistock to verify some of her stories."

"Good. You shall have the car for as long as you like. I see that you officers from the Yard go the same way to work as us in Devonshire. You look first for the motive. We've not been idle while you've been away. Dr. Fraser and Dr. Symon have made their reports, which don't coincide with the evidence Dr. Symon gave at the inquest. However, that needn't concern us; it's a matter for the coroner. What does concern us is that the medical evidence leaves the question of foul play open and we can go ahead. Of course in a place like this, it's impossible to keep things out of the papers. There was a paragraph in both the Plymouth papers this morning and the reporters came here for further details. I had to tell them something. I said it was quite true that there were some further developments and that, at the request of the Chief Constable, two officers from Scotland Yard had been detailed to help us, but that it was no good trying to interview them; they were far too busy. If I hadn't talked to them straight, they would have printed all kinds of fantastic stories."

"I think that was very wise of you, Mr. Carstairs. And now to business. Which of your officers knows Moorstead best?"

"Oh, Inspector Viggers has known Moorstead man and boy for more than thirty years. As a matter of fact, he was born there."

"Can I see him this evening, do you think?"

"Yes; as it happens he's in the station now to draw the pay. Step into my office and I'll send him in."

Inspector Viggers was a weather-beaten man with a red face and sandy hair; a little slow of speech and perhaps of apprehension. He looked like a moor man in uniform. If he had ever been trained in gymnastics and marching, he had forgotten what he was taught.

"Inspector Viggers?" asked Richardson.

"Yes, sir."

"You know Moorstead well?"

"I ought to, sir; I ought to know every stone in the place."

"And every man, woman and child there."

Viggers took time to consider this question before he replied, "Pretty near, sir."

"You know the people living in Sun Lane?"

A slow smile dawned on the rugged countenance—a smile of reminiscence. "Yes, sir—most of them."

"What sort of people live there?"

"They're the poorest people in the town, but that doesn't mean that they're all criminals. They're just—poor."

"Do you know Mrs. Duke?"

"Yes, sir; she's had a hard life since her husband died, bringing up those children. If she hadn't let lodgings she couldn't have paid her way."

"But now she keeps a car."

The smile dawned again. "You'd scarce call it a car, sir; there's a driving-seat to it, but that's all. It belongs to that boy of hers, and how he raised the money to buy it second-hand I can't tell you. He says he's making a profit on it by taking it out with market produce, but he's down sick at home just now."

"Then who drives the car when he's sick?"

"Not his sister—she's no licence and couldn't drive it if she had. I expect the car's laid up."

"Would you give the Duke family a good mark for honesty?"

Again the inspector looked at his boots for inspiration. "Yes, sir, I should. The daughter Susie is a wonderful talker; she'd talk the hind leg off a donkey when doing a deal, but she wouldn't rob you."

"Have you ever come across their lodger, Dick Pengelly, who was quarry-smith at the Red Quarry?"

"Yes, sir; he's one of them Cornish Labour agitators that's always trying to stir up trouble. There's no harm in him except his tongue. Everybody knows him in Moorstead and most of the folk are fed-up with him. He used to try and get up meetings in the market-place on Sundays, but he had to give it up because the people said, 'Why, it's only Dick Pengelly,' and they wouldn't stop to listen to him. But I hear that his boss has fired him and he's gone off to find another job."

"He was a quarrelsome man, I suppose?"

The inspector searched his memory. "No...no, I wouldn't call him that. He was just an agitator because he was born that way."

"Thank you, Inspector, that was all I wanted to ask you."

"Very good, sir. Perhaps I ought to tell you that in Sun Lane they've been saying that Pengelly was courting the Duke girl." He stopped for a moment to see how this piece of intelligence was received, then turned on his heel and left the room.

Sergeant Jago came in to know whether Richardson was ready for supper and bed at the hotel. As they walked down together, Jago inquired whether his chief had got anything useful out of Inspector Viggers of Moorstead.

"Nothing to speak of, except that in Sun Lane, where tongues run wild, Pengelly was believed to be paying court to Susie Duke."

"Ah!" said Jago. "That's why she wouldn't tell us all she knew about his whereabouts. She was shielding him, which shows that he must have been guilty of something. And he had a motive for the murder."

"It's too early in the proceedings to be making up your mind against anyone, as I think you'll find out before you're much older."

Richardson had trained himself to dismiss his cases from his mind as soon as he got into bed, but that night he broke his good resolution and lay awake pondering. Pengelly was among the "possibles," but would Pengelly, when on the tramp looking for work, be carrying a heavy walking-stick which obviously would have cost him something to buy? A "swanky" stick; and would a quarryman be carrying a walking-stick, anyhow? And then why would he be a quarter of a mile or more out of his way? Rowe's Quarry lay on the road into Tavistock, which meant going right through Duketon, and if he wanted to waylay Dearborn he could have done it just as easily on the road between Moorstead and Duketon. It was a puzzle whichever way you looked at it. The first thing to be done was to locate that motor-lorry in Tavistock, and the second to find out whether Pengelly had applied to be taken on in Rowe's Quarry. Perhaps it was this decision that brought sleep to Richardson's eyelids, for beyond the Pengelly clue everything was cloudy and mysterious.

When the two Scotland Yard officers met at their early breakfast-table next morning there was no change of plan. Sergeant Jago went off to arrange about the police car while Richardson smoked his pipe in the bar parlour. Twelve minutes after the car pulled up at the hotel door they were in Tavistock in Jago's own hunting-ground, making the round of the repairing-shops. News flies fast among the garage hands in a little town, and Sergeant Jago was quickly directed to a little shop only recently opened. Beside a few derelict cars with dismantled engines there stood the tiniest of motor-lorries with a driving-seat and a flat platform behind it. A mechanic in blue overalls was stretched on the floor beneath it, tinkering with the brake bands. Hearing voices he protruded a head and blew his nose on an oily piece of cotton waste. Seeing possible customers he writhed out from under the car and asked what he could do for the visitors.

"We've looked in to see young Duke's lorry from Moorstead," explained Jago. "Is that it?"

"Yes, there she is, and I'm wondering how long she's to be left here. She's all ready for the road. I was just looking at her brakes when you come in."

"Who left her here?"

"Why, the young lady, Ernie Duke's sister, and the bloke that was driving her."

"Who was that?"

"I'm sure I dunno who he was. The young lady called him 'Dick.' He said that her brother was laid up in Moorstead, but that as soon as he got better he'd come down and drive her away."

Richardson picked up the thread of the conversation. "We were wondering what sort of a driver the man was who brought her in."

The mechanic laughed sourly. "I'll show you the kind of driver he was. See that door?" He pointed to the wooden gate through which vehicles had to drive. "See that scar in the paint? He made that bringing her in. He took the turn too short out of the street and grazed the lamp-post with his bumper, and then lost his head and went into my gate. If I hadn't shouted to him to stop he'd have scraped the gate on the other side, too. He got down then and let me drive her in. It's my belief that it was the first time in his life he'd ever had a steering-wheel in his hand."

"What sort of man was he to look at?"

"Oh, a wiry sort of chap of about forty, I should say. I'd have put him down as a garage mechanic to judge by the state of his hands if it hadn't been for the way he drove the car in."

"Well, we'll let Mr. Duke know that his car's ready and I dare say he'll be along to fetch her. What day was it they left her?"

"She's been here ten days. I understood she was to have been fetched away the next day."

"Well, we'll remind him about it. Good day."

The two officers stopped a moment to consult before they reached the car.

"Ten days," said Richardson; "that brings us to the day of the murder, but it doesn't bring us any nearer to Pengelly, for what would he be doing with a walking-stick in the driving-seat of that little runabout, encumbered by that young woman?"

"But why did she tell lies about it? Why didn't she own up that Pengelly drove her into Tavistock?"

Richardson pointed mutely to a deep scratch on the paint-work of the lamp-post and to the scar on the garage gate. "If you'd been sitting beside a man who'd never driven a car in his life before and had no licence you wouldn't boast about it, would you?"

"Ah! Then you think that she was afraid it would come out that Pengelly was driving without a licence?"

"Yes, and I think, too, that he avoided taking the direct route through Duketon for fear of being stopped by the local constable. That's why he drove through Sandiland into Tavistock."

"You don't think there was any more serious reason for that girl lying to us?"

"At present I don't, but if we can find Pengelly in Rowe's Quarry, we may get down to something like the truth." He gave the order to the police driver to take them to Rowe's Quarry.

Chapter Five

Rowe's Quarry was a much more extensive place than the little quarry near Moorstead. It had been worked for many years; the grey granite of which it is composed is to be found all over the district in churches, public halls and private houses, because it is the hardest and most durable stone in the west of England.

A foreman met the two detectives at the gate, which he opened a little unwillingly in response to Richardson's assurance that they were police officers come to make inquiries. The foreman led the way to his office, which was partitioned off from one of the sheds where the stone-dressing was done. Conversation had to be conducted to the musical ring of steel upon steel.

"Have you taken on recently a quarry-smith called Dick Pengelly?"

"Not as a quarry-smith, but I've taken on trial a man of that name as a smith's striker and he's shaping very well."

"Can we have a few words with him?"

"Yes, but don't keep him too long. We happen to be full up with orders just now."

Jago intervened. "Couldn't you turn on another man to take his place? There must be lots who can use a hammer."

"Right; if you'll stay here I'll send him in."

While they waited, Richardson was busy with a literary composition of his own: before him lay the two photographs of the anonymous letters. When a knock at the door announced their man he covered the photographs quickly with a sheet of official foolscap.

The arch agitator did not look at all the kind of man they were expecting. He was a wiry, sharp-featured little fellow with a hunted expression in his eyes. Evidently he had been told by the foreman the quality of his visitors; he was on the defensive.

Richardson pulled out a stool from under the desk and said cheerfully, "Sit down there, Pengelly." He knew the value of placing a suspect at a lower level than himself.

"I'd rather stand."

"If you don't mind I'd rather you sat down, because we've several questions to ask you and you'll answer them more comfortably sitting than standing. Last Saturday week you drove young Mr. Duke's lorry from Moorstead into Tavistock, didn't you?"

"I went in Duke's lorry, if that's what you mean?"

"Yes, that's what we mean. You went in the lorry, sitting at the steering-wheel."

Pengelly seemed about to protest, but Richardson went on smoothly, "And instead of coming the nearest way to the quarry to look for work, you turned off on the road to Sandiland and left the lorry at that little garage in North Street, Tavistock, to be kept till called for."

"You seem to know all about it."

"We do know something about it. For example, we can tell you why you didn't take the direct road up through the village of Duketon. It was because there's a constable posted there and you were driving without a licence."

Pengelly became defiant. "Oh, if that's all I was driving without a licence, but I dare say now that I've got a job the fine won't break me."

"I don't know what the Bench gives down here for driving without a licence, but if you like to own up in a statement, I'll see that it's brought to the notice of the magistrate. Here, pull up your stool to this desk and write it out yourself: 'I, Richard Pengelly, feel it my duty to admit that on September 29 I drove a motor-lorry from Moorstead to Tavistock on business but I had no accident.' And sign it."

Pengelly hesitated; he was no penman, but whether it was this fact or that he scented a trap Richardson was unable to determine. He banked on the former explanation.

"You needn't worry about the handwriting or spelling. The great thing is to get it down in your own handwriting."

With his tongue protruding from the corner of his mouth, and breathing heavily, Pengelly set himself to the task. At last it was done and Richardson turned to another aspect of that lorry drive.

"You had a young lady with you in the lorry—young Duke's sister. I wonder you didn't let her drive."

Pengelly was taken off his guard. "She'd got no licence either. Her brother wouldn't ever let her drive."

"Oh, that was it? If anybody was to get into trouble it wasn't to be her. It does you credit, Pengelly. Now, when you turned off towards Sandilands hadn't you another motive? You knew that it was about the time when Mr. Dearborn was due to come along in his car on his way to Winterton, and naturally you had a strong motive for telling him what you thought of him before leaving the district."

"I didn't want to see the man again. Why should I?"

"To have the last word. We all like to do that when we have a legitimate grievance, and he had sacked you without a character."

Pengelly flushed with angry reminiscence. "If I'd seen him I'd have told him off, I dare say, but I didn't."

"No, but you saw his car standing at the Duchy Hotel, so you thought of waiting for him down the road."

Pengelly's hands clenched; the hunted look returned to his eyes. "I wasn't going to waste my time waiting for a swine like that."

"So you just drove on and left him at the Duchy Hotel?"

"Yes."

"You know that he had an accident on the way down Sandiland Hill and was picked up unconscious?"

"I heard something about it."

"Thank you, Pengelly. That's all I want to ask you for the present."

When they were alone Jago remarked, "That man was lying."

"Up to a point he was telling the truth, I think."

"Yes, because you dragged it out of him, but what puzzles me, Mr. Richardson, is how you knew that Dearborn had left his car standing outside the Duchy Hotel."

"I didn't know it. It was just a lucky shot."

"And that statement you got him to make? It struck me that you worded it in a funny way."

"That was because you didn't notice that it had one or two of the words used in those anonymous letters. I wanted to get a specimen of his handwriting; that was all. Now let's have a look at his statement and compare it with the photographs of the letters." Richardson laid the three documents on the table and pored over them. He shook his head. "No. Pengelly never wrote those letters. He spells 'business' right; not 'bisness' as in both anonymous letters. Then look at the word 'accident'—it's in much heavier writing than the same word in the letter to the Chief Constable."

"I see that. But it never entered my head that he was the writer of the anonymous letters. I think we've got him cold on the murder, though; he had a motive—he admits that he saw

Dearborn's car standing outside the Duchy Hotel. He went down the road to wait for him. Short of absolute proof what more can you want?"

"We haven't done with our inquiries yet. Here comes the foreman. Pack up these papers quick. I don't want him to see them."

"Well, gentlemen," said the foreman, "how did Pengelly shape when you put him through the hoop?"

"He admitted driving a car without a licence, and I suppose that the county police will have something to say about that. Otherwise he came out all right. I'm sorry to have taken up your time. We may have to see him again to clear up one or two minor points in his statement, but not for a few days. If he's a competent workman, in your place I should keep him on. Good day."

They entered the police car and Richardson gave the order to drive to the Duchy Hotel, Duketon. The driver went like the wind, covering the five miles in six minutes. The officers jumped down, entered the bar and asked to see the manager.

"Police officers, are you?" questioned this functionary. "I don't remember seeing either of you before."

"No?" said Richardson. "Well, we won't waste time over explanations. I have a simple question to ask you. Did Mr. Dearborn, who was injured in a motor accident last Saturday week and has since died, call in at this hotel late in the afternoon?"

"Lord! I thought when I saw you that you were gentlemen of the Press. Is that the new wheeze—to call yourselves police officers? I suppose you represent the London newspapers. You'll find a couple of your colleagues of the Plymouth Press in the bar parlour. I see the papers want to make a mystery out of that poor gentleman's death; they're not content with the verdict of the coroner's jury."

"We've nothing to do with the Press. As I told you we're police officers; you might oblige me by answering my question."

"I shall have to ask my barmaid for the answer. I don't see everybody that calls in for a drink, but she'll know. Laura! The last time you saw Mr. Dearborn, did he have any refreshment?"

The lady behind the bar searched her memory.

"He had a cup of tea, Mr. Tovey; you see it was about four o'clock in the afternoon—a cup of tea and a biscuit."

"Thank you, Mr. Tovey, that's all we wanted to ask."

The licensee followed them out to the door in his anxiety to be helpful and watched them enter the car.

"Now," said Richardson, "the next thing we have to do is to tackle that young woman in Sun Lane and she'll need some careful handling, because I believe that she has the key to the whole mystery. I shouldn't wonder myself to find that Viggers was right and that she's in love with that fellow Pengelly."

"Then she won't give him away."

"She won't if she can help it." Richardson leaned forward to speak to the driver. "You might put us down at the top of the lane and then I want you to go the round of the shops where they sell walking-sticks and see whether they stock any like the one that was picked up on the scene of the crime. You saw it, I suppose?"

"Yes, and I've had it in my hand, too."

"Then, as we may be some time in Sun Lane, you'd better go in and have your dinner."

Doors and windows were clear of heads this time as the two officers made their way to the dwelling of the Dukes, or, as Detective Sergeant Jago phrased it, to the "Dukeries."

"Isn't this going to be an awkward hour for calling on the young woman, Mr. Richardson—if they're at dinner, I mean?"

"They dine early in these parts. Perhaps you're right. We had better go and get our own sandwiches, and catch Miss Susie Duke when she's full fed and at peace with the world."

They retraced their steps and stopped at a little tea-shop a hundred yards from the opening into Sun Lane. They ordered tea and scones and Richardson laid his watch on the table.

"We'll give them another twenty minutes," he said.

"I'm wondering how you're going to begin your questioning, Mr. Richardson," said Jago.

"That will depend upon the young lady and how she receives us. I never look ahead too far. The great point in questioning women is to feel one's way and not antagonize them. If you do that they turn mulish and you get nothing out of them."

Jago munched his scone, ruminating. "It seems to me that the questioning of witnesses and getting statements from them is one of the fine arts," he said at last.

"Psha! It's a question only of being quick in the uptake and knowing something about the case before you begin. I mean to play upon the tender spot that this young woman has in her heart for her late lodger. If I have any luck I believe that something will come out that will surprise you." He looked at the watch lying on the table. "The time's nearly up. Swallow your tea while I pay the bill."

As they walked down the lane they saw through open doors that the housewives were busy at their kitchen sinks and that their daughters were carrying out scraps to the poultry in the back-yards. They pushed on to the "Dukeries" and knocked at the door. Mrs. Duke, with her sleeves turned up and a rough canvas apron on to protect her dress, opened the door. She recoiled in alarm at the sight of her visitors.

"Why, you are the same police officers that called yesterday. Is it about the lorry?"

"We have called to see your daughter, Mrs. Duke. There is nothing to be alarmed about. Perhaps you will kindly call her."

"I don't know that she's not gone out."

"I hope not, Mrs. Duke, because that would mean that we should have to wait in the lane outside until she came in, and that might set the neighbours talking."

"Well, I'll go and see whether I can find her, if you'll stop here."

The search was successful; footsteps were heard again upon the stairs and Miss Susie Duke bustled in, dressed in her best walking-suit with its rabbit-skin necklet and her latest hat. She nodded to him with a smile; her last experience with detectives having been that they were easy to bluff.

"We've called about that drive you took in your brother's lorry on the 29th of last month, Miss Duke—the time you took it into Tavistock. Never mind what you told us before; people are apt to make mistakes when they are first questioned by police officers. Now that you've had time to think things over I'm sure you'll see that it's best to tell the truth," said Richardson.

"I don't remember what I told you last time."

"I'm sure you don't, and I'm sure that you don't want Dick Pengelly to get into worse trouble than he's in already for driving a car without a licence."

To Richardson's surprise the girl changed colour and seemed about to burst into tears. "I ought to tell you, my dear," he said, "that we've seen Dick Pengelly and that he's made a clean breast of it—that he drove the lorry without a licence with you sitting at his side; that you took the road to Tavistock through Sandiland. He made a written statement which I have here and I want you to do the same; then the case of driving without a licence will be quite cleared up."

"Where is he?"

"Oh, he's all right. He's got a job as a smith's striker in Rowe's Quarry near Tavistock."

The girl seemed to be immensely relieved by this intelligence. "I didn't want him to get into trouble on my account," she faltered. "I ought not to have let him drive."

"If the county police prosecute him for driving without a licence it's not a very serious offence, and as he said, he can easily pay the fine out of his wages. Now, about this statement of yours; it can be quite short. I'll dictate it for you if you like." Richardson turned back the tablecloth and opened his attaché-case to get out writing materials. "Now take this chair, Miss Duke, and don't worry any more about it."

The girl hesitated; it was one thing to use her tongue, but quite another to commit words to paper. "I'd sooner not write anything. I'm quite ready to answer your questions, but not to stick things down on paper."

"That's a pity," said Richardson with a sigh, beginning to return paper and ink to his writing-case. "I thought you would have been glad to help Pengelly."

"How would my statement help him?"

"Well, by confirming what he told me. But of course if you won't, you won't, and for all I know to the contrary the police may bring other charges against him—far more serious charges."

The girl moved to the chair. "What do you want me to write?"

"Only a few words which I'll dictate to you if you like. 'I, Susan Duke, feel it my duty to admit that on September 29 last, having business to do in Tavistock, I allowed Richard Pengelly to drive my brother's lorry into Tavistock though he had no driving-licence, and I went with him.' Then sign it. You see, it's nothing very dreadful."

The girl took up the pen, saying, "Go ahead then." She wrote rapidly and signed her name with a flourish.

Chapter Six

Richardson picked up the statement and examined it. The word "business" was written "bisness" just as it was in the letter to the Commissioner; the handwriting, too, was obviously the same as in both anonymous letters.

"I've seen this handwriting somewhere before, Miss Duke. Yes, and the same kind of spelling, too. I see you spell 'business!' 'bisness!'"

"Lots of people do that," said the girl defiantly.

"Yes. I've seen it spelt like that by someone who wrote to Scotland Yard. I have a photograph of the letter here." He fumbled among the papers in his writing-case. "Here you are. You see, the letter has been photographed, and for the matter of that so has another anonymous letter addressed to the Superintendent of Police at Winterton. And now, almost by accident, I have the writer of both letters before me."

"I don't know what you mean."

"Then let me make my meaning clearer. You were ready to tell untruths to the police when it was only a question of driving without a licence, but when it came to murder you didn't want to see a murderer go unpunished. You couldn't come forward openly, because you were afraid that the police might fix the crime on Dick Pengelly, since he had a legitimate grievance against the murdered man. Wasn't that it?"

The girl made no reply. She stared at the floor.

"I think we understand each other now," said Richardson, "and I feel sure that your best way to help Pengelly is to tell us the whole truth about what you saw that afternoon. Pengelly has already told us that he saw Mr. Dearborn's car standing outside the Duchy Hotel. No doubt he pointed it out to you."

The bravado was not crushed out of her. "You think yourself very clever, don't you? But there's nothing to show that I wrote those letters." She picked up the photograph of the letter addressed to the Chief Constable of Scotland Yard from Tavistock. "Why, look here, the writing in this letter is sloping backwards. The other isn't."

"It isn't."

"Well then, how can you have the face to fix the writing on me?"

"Only because if you were to copy this letter in a hand sloping backwards, your writing would be just like this. People can't disguise their handwriting by sloping words backwards. No, Miss Susie, you committed no offence by writing the letters; on the contrary you were doing your best to help the police. Why not help them a little further? You don't want a murderer to get off, do you? You don't want people to try to attribute the murder to Dick Pengelly. Why not tell us the whole story, exactly as it happened?"

"I suppose you thought it was a clever game to trap me into making that written statement. All you wanted was to get a specimen of my handwriting. It was a dirty trick."

"Well you see, Miss Duke, we had to get evidence as to who wrote these anonymous letters because the writer, whoever she was, was likely to be an important witness in the case. You think that we are trying to fasten the guilt on to Dick Pengelly. You're quite wrong. I, for one, don't believe that he had anything to do with the murder and I'll tell you why. The weapon used was a heavy walking-stick with a silver band round it—not the kind of stick that a quarryman would care to buy—and that rules out Pengelly as the man who struck Dearborn. As an eye-witness you are in a position to support my view, and so you ought not to hold anything back."

"My! But aren't you detectives clever to think of that walking-stick being a way of clearing Dick Pengelly!" There was real admiration in her voice now. "Very well, I'll tell you the truth and you can believe it or not as you like. Dick didn't want to drive through Duketon; the policeman there hasn't enough to do and so he's a busybody, always poking his nose into other people's affairs."

"Why did Pengelly drive the lorry at all if he hadn't a licence?"

"Well, you see, my brother was going to drive him into Tavistock with his luggage to look for a job there. But when Ernie was taken ill he said, 'It's rotten luck for you, but why shouldn't you take the lorry and drive her yourself, with Susie to keep you on the right road. She has to go to Tavistock to get the money the fruiterer owes me. You can leave the lorry at the garage for me to call for when I'm better.'"

"But when you turned off towards Sandiland it wasn't only because Pengelly was afraid of the Duketon constable. He must have had another reason."

"Well, as soon as he saw Mr. Dearborn's car, he thought he'd stop him down the road and tell him off, so we drove on down the hill a bit of the way, parked the lorry there, well into the roadside, and then him and me went back up the hill to a place where we got a clear view of the top. We got off the road and sat down among the heather to wait for Mr. Dearborn. Dick says to me, 'As soon as his car comes in sight I'll step out into the middle of the road and hold up my arms; that'll stop him; he won't dare drive over me.'"

"And then?"

"Well, then a funny thing happened. Just as Mr. Dearborn's car came in sight on the top of the hill, another chap jumped out of the heather and stuck out his arms just like Dick meant to, and he had a whacking great stick in his hand. He didn't see us."

"What happened then?"

"It was all so quick that it was difficult to see exactly. Mr. Dearborn jumped out of his car with the starting-handle in his hand, and there was a bit of a set-to between them. I saw the fellow with the stick bring it down with a whack on Mr. Dearborn's head, and I saw Mr. Dearborn drop the starting-handle. The man picked it up and threw it into the heather. He'd broken his stick and he threw the pieces away, after the starting-handle. Then he made off down into the gully, and there was Mr. Dearborn lying beside the car."

"Didn't you go up the hill to help him?"

"I wanted to, but Dick wouldn't let me. He said, 'They'll blame me for this, that's certain. We must get out of it as quick as we can and keep our mouths shut.' And he took me by the arm and dragged me down to the lorry. I don't believe we spoke a word till we got well-nigh into Tavistock."

"What made you write the anonymous letters?"

"I knew one of the jurymen at the inquest, and he told me that they'd brought it in as death from an accident. Well then I thought, 'Here's a pretty state of affairs. A man's murdered in broad daylight on the moor and the murderer gets away with it. It might be our turn next.' So I just sat down and dropped a line to the Superintendent. And then when I thought what a slow lot they were in Winterton, I dropped a line to the big man in Scotland Yard."

"But you posted one letter in Moorstead and the other in Tavistock."

"That's right. A friend of mine was going that way and I asked him for a lift. I wanted to find Dick Pengelly and get him to come with me to the police. I tried the garage, but they'd never seen him since the day we left the car there. So I bought a sheet of paper and an envelope and a stamp and wrote the letter in a tea-shop and posted it."

Sergeant Jago had been making notes of her admissions and was embodying them in the form of a statement. Richardson read this over to her.

"Lord! I didn't know that I'd told you all that," said she; "but it's gospel truth."

"You don't want to add anything?"

"No."

"Then will you sign it?"

"What! Sign another statement?"

"Yes. The first would be no use in a court of law."

"Do you mean that you're going to have me up as a witness?"

"Not until we catch the man who used the stick. When we do catch him, both you and Pengelly will be wanted to give evidence."

"You mean I'll have to go to Exeter Assizes and swear to all this and have my picture taken in the newspapers and be badgered by a barrister in a wig?"

"You'll get all your expenses paid by the Crown."

"I dare say. You'll be telling me next that the King will want me to come up to Buckingham Palace to be thanked for what I've done. No, I tell you straight; it's not good enough."

"It's the duty of everyone to do what is best for the country. None of us want murderers to be at large."

"When I told you all this, it was because you'd told me about that walking-stick and somehow, I don't know why, I trust you, though you are a policeman, and I'm sure you'll do your best to keep Dick Pengelly out of this business, because you know as well as I do that he had no hand in it. Now then, where am I to sign?"

Richardson indicated the place, blotted the ink and stowed away his writing materials. "You've nothing to fear, my girl, and I'm sure that we are all very much obliged to you. Good-bye."

They found the police car waiting at the corner of the lane.

"Have you had any luck?" asked Richardson.

"No, Chief Inspector. I've been round to every shop where they sell walking-sticks; they all told me the same thing. The only place where you would be likely to find a stick like that would be in Plymouth or Exeter. You wouldn't even find one in Tavistock."

"Good. Then we've cleared up one point. Now we had better get back to Winterton."

Richardson found Superintendent Carstairs in his office.

"You've been busy to-day," said the Superintendent.

"Yes, Mr. Carstairs; we have. We've seen Pengelly, and we've cleared up the question as to who wrote those anonymous letters. It was a young woman in Moorstead."

"The devil it was! Who is she?"

"The daughter of the woman with whom Pengelly lodged."

"What was her object in writing them?"

"She has made a long written statement which I have here. You had better read it."

The Superintendent read the statement and shook his head over it. "All the way through she has apparently been shielding Pengelly. Perhaps there's a love-affair between them?"

"I think there is."

"Well then, this statement of hers is so much waste paper. You know what women are, Mr. Richardson, quite as well as I do. They do the wildest things when they're in love."

"They do, but what motive could she have had in writing those letters if they weren't true? All she had to do, if she wanted to shield Pengelly, was to keep her mouth shut. Then there's the question of that walking-stick. We got the driver of your car to make a round of the shops in Moorstead where sticks are sold, and the answer was always the same—that you can't buy a stick like that nearer than Plymouth or Exeter."

Carstairs stroked his beard. "Everything points to Pengelly having been the guilty one—motive, opportunity and character. All the girl does is to introduce another character and make him do exactly what she saw Pengelly do. As for the stick, it may have belonged to the murdered man himself; he could have bought it in Plymouth when he went to the bank there, or he may have had it for years. I don't want to queer your pitch, Chief Inspector, but if the case were mine, and there was any danger of Pengelly clearing out of the county, I should lay him by the heels on the charge of motoring without a licence, and see whether the truth couldn't be shaken out of him."

"It's perfectly open to you to do that, Mr. Carstairs, because I shall have to interview him again and put the girl's statement to him. He only told us a quarter of the truth. I should also like to see the widow and ask her whether her late husband possessed a stick such as the broken one."

Superintendent Carstairs had his full share of the dogged obstinacy that is found among South Devon men. "If you'll excuse my saying so, Mr. Richardson, I think you're giving yourself a lot of unnecessary trouble."

"I hope not, Superintendent, because I should be very sorry to see you take some step which you would afterwards regret. Of course, you haven't had the advantage of sizing up the girl when interviewing her, as I did."

"Still, I don't think that the question of that stick is sufficient to clear Pengelly."

"There's another factor in my mind. Don't you think that if Pengelly had attacked Dearborn after holding up his car, Dearborn would have complained to the police as soon as he recovered consciousness?"

"After a crack on the head like that you can never tell how much a man remembers."

"But Mr. Dearborn was not suffering from loss of memory; he invented a story for his wife's benefit, that the brakes had refused to act. Yet Sergeant Jago found the brakes in perfect order. Don't you think the girl's story is supported by the fact that Dearborn was anxious to conceal all indications of the attack made upon him? You must remember that he has been mysterious about his past ever since he came to Devonshire. He may have recognized in his assailant some private enemy of whom we know nothing."

"That's all very well, but it will mean that we have to go chasing all over England for a mystery man, when we have the real assailant right under our noses."

Richardson tactfully changed the subject. "Did the funeral take place to-day?"

"No, it's fixed for to-morrow morning."

"And the doctors' report? What did the coroner think of it?"

"Oh, he took the line that now the Yard was investigating the case, there was no need to hold a second inquest. The doctors' report says clearly that the deceased received a heavy blow on the head from a blunt instrument which fractured the skull, which was unusually thin, and that the injury could not have been caused by the head coming into contact with the roof of the car."

"If the funeral is to be to-morrow, Mr. Carstairs, I should be glad if you would have a telephone message sent to the manager of the Union Bank, who is sole executor to the will. After the funeral he would read the will to the widow."

"Certainly I will."

"In the meantime I hope that Mrs. Dearborn will not take it amiss if I call on her this evening to ask her about that stick; whether her late husband ever had one like it."

"I'm sure she will not object, but what I want to know is whether you intend to question Pengelly at the quarry, or whether you would like me to have him brought down here on the charge of driving without a licence."

"Wouldn't the procedure be by summons?"

"Not in this case, because there is the danger of the defendant moving out of the jurisdiction."

Richardson considered. He had to decide in his own mind whether Pengelly would be more communicative as a free man in the quarry than when in custody in a police station. He had to make up his mind quickly.

"Yes, Mr. Carstairs, I should be glad if you would have him brought in. Perhaps you would instruct your officers to tell the foreman that he's wanted only for a motoring offence. And now, if you'll allow me, I'll go and see Mrs. Dearborn."

He found the lady engaged in her back garden. She had heard the front-door bell and was on her way to receive her visitor. "You must be surprised to find me gardening, Mr. Richardson, but I find that it takes my mind off all this sadness and trouble."

"I have really come to ask you one question only—whether your husband had a heavy walking-stick with a crook handle and a silver band?"

She shook her head. "No, he had only one walking-stick. Come into the house and I'll show it to you. He never used it after he got the car."

She showed him a stick of light-coloured wood, which was standing with the umbrellas in the hall. "Have you found out anything more?"

"Yes, we've found out who sent the anonymous letters, but don't let us speak of them now. What I want to get from you is exactly what happened when Dr. Wilson brought your husband here after his accident?"

"Dr. Wilson helped him into the house. He seemed very weak. The doctor said that he ought to be got to bed as soon as possible, and that our own doctor should be sent for. I got my husband upstairs and into bed after washing off the blood from his neck."

"Was he delirious or confused in his talk?"

"Not at all. He spoke quite rationally, but his voice was weak. I told him I was going to send for Dr. Symon and he refused to allow me. I looked in upon him two or three times during the night; he seemed to be sleeping heavily. In the morning I took him some tea, but he scarcely touched it. He was quite sensible, though. I begged him again to see the doctor, but he wouldn't. He asked me to bring up his cheque-book from his writing-table, and then when I next visited him he made me sit down and said, 'I'm getting fed-up with this place, and if you don't mind staying here by yourself for a bit, here's a cheque for you for £200.' I haven't cashed the cheque, but it's drawn on the Union Bank and the handwriting isn't a bit shaky. He went on to say that he would go away for a bit and look for a place and then send for me."

"When he made this extraordinary suggestion did you think he was light-headed?"

"I did, but his manner was so calm and natural that it was difficult to think that he was raving. I tried to soothe him by saying that I would help him to pack as soon as he felt well enough. Then for the next two days he scarcely spoke to me. I took in his meals, but he didn't touch them. He lay practically the whole day in a state of coma. I got so frightened that I called in Dr. Symon off my own bat, and he attended him until the last."

"Did your husband seem quite clear as to how the accident occurred?"

"He seemed to remember it perfectly. He said that when coming down the hill his brakes refused to act, and at a curve in the road the car swerved into the ditch."

"You are sure he made no mention of anyone stopping the car and attacking him?"

"I am quite sure. Since your visit this morning I've been thinking things over and suggesting to myself that he was light-headed, but though, naturally, his voice was weak and he was suffering from his head, I feel more certain than ever that his mind and his memory were clear. After you had left this morning I did think of going round to see Dr. Symon, but as you had the case in hand I decided that it would be better to leave everything to you."

Richardson rose. "I must apologize for making this second visit, Mrs. Dearborn. You may be quite sure that I shall do my best to get to the bottom of the mystery."

Chapter Seven

RICHARDSON declined the offer of tea on the ground that his work would not allow him time for accepting such invitations. Mrs. Dearborn saw him to the gate. At that moment, Chance decreed that he should make the acquaintance of her only friend in Winterton. A tall young man, striding along the road, lifted his hat to Mrs. Dearborn and was passing on when she called to him:

"I should like you to know Lieutenant Cosway. Mr. Cosway, let me introduce this gentleman who has come all the way from London to deal with my affairs. Mr. Richardson is a Chief Inspector from Scotland Yard."

Cosway recoiled in mock horror. "I'd like to shake hands with you, Mr. Richardson, if you'll give me time to run over certain incidents in my past life."

"That's all right, sir; I've received no instructions to inquire into your biography."

"Perhaps Mr. Richardson will tell you that there's a complication over the medical evidence at the inquest."

To Richardson this chance informal meeting with the one man in Winterton who knew Mrs. Dearborn was a godsend. "Are you going my way, sir?"

"Yes; I was going to the golf club, but I would far rather spend the time having a talk with you."

They saluted Mrs. Dearborn and set off in company.

"What's the complication, Mr. Richardson? Surely the facts about Dearborn's death were fully cleared up at the inquest?"

"I may tell you confidentially, Mr. Cosway, that from information since received we have reason to believe that Mr. Dearborn owed his fatal injury not to the motor accident, but to a blow on the head inflicted by some assailant."

"Good God! I can't say that I'm altogether surprised. I have always told my people that the late lamented Dearborn had a past—a lurider past even than mine—and that was why he behaved like an ill-mannered bear when people tried to be friendly with him."

"Has Mrs. Dearborn told you that since the accident he talked of leaving the neighbourhood for good?"

"No, but he *has* left it for good; he's gone to a land where people don't go chasing one another with hatchets, or so the parson tells us on Sundays. But I see the whole thing. The lust for gold tempted the deceased Dearborn from the straight and narrow path, and as one can't dig up gold in one's own back garden he had to help himself to another fellow's pile and was hiding down here in the wilds of Devon; and then, Nemesis, or whatever the lady was called, set about squaring the account and arranged that the hiding-place should be divulged and there you are. Did Nemesis use a revolver for the job?"

"No, Mr. Cosway; nothing but a walking-stick."

"How flat and unfilmlike. But joking apart, I'm really sorry for that poor lonely woman and I'd like to do something to help her. As soon as the funeral is over my mother intends to call upon her. She didn't do it before because we were afraid that that bounder of a man might be rude to her."

Richardson knew from earlier experience that young naval officers of this type could be supremely useful, and that in any case when one got below the instinct for treating serious subjects lightly one found real sterling virtues.

"I must confess that we are not getting on as fast as I could have wished, and I feel sure that if you would consent to help me in unravelling the mystery of Dearborn's past life, something useful might come of it."

The jesting imp resumed its sway for a moment.

"To think that I should be invited to share the secrets of the Yard has taken my breath away. They will spot me as the bogy man next time I enter the mess-room in Devonport. Something in my sinuous walk will betray me."

Richardson smiled. "I haven't noticed anything sinuous about you, so far, Mr. Cosway; but seriously I feel sure that you can help us. Any detail about Dearborn's behaviour, social or otherwise, may be useful."

At this point his new acquaintance stopped dead and gripped him by the arm. "Good Lord! How did I come to forget it? Last Sunday, just as I was going off to the golf club, I was stopped in the road by a hobbledehoy youth who asked me if I knew where a Mr. Dearborn lived—he wanted to see him. I said, 'There's the house but you're too late to see him—he died last night.' The boy turned pale green and made off in the direction of the station without another word."

"How was he dressed?"

"Oh, something like a city clerk in his best clothes, I should say."

"Would you know him again if you saw him?"

"Yes, I think I should; for one thing his face was smothered in freckles."

"Didn't he ask when the funeral was to be?"

"No; he seemed quite broken up by the news of Dearborn's death. You see what this means, Mr. Richardson? That poor boy was the illegitimate son of the dead man. He'd come down to touch the hard heart of his parent and stick him for a handsome little sum as the price of his silence. And there he was on the wrong side by more than thirty shillings for his return railway fare. He left my heart bleeding for him."

"If we could get hold of that young man…or if we could get to know something about Dearborn…"

"I've told you all that anyone here knows about him—that he was a surly brute who wanted to keep himself to himself."

"Thank you, Mr. Cosway. Our roads part here. I must be getting back to my work."

"They call our house The Elms, in case you want me. I believe that the purveyors of milk, meat and vegetables have a less flattering name for it. However, 'The Elms' is painted on the gate. Good-bye."

Richardson betook himself to the police station where he found Sergeant Jago gossiping with the police patrol.

"Anything fresh, Mr. Richardson?" inquired Jago.

"Step into the Superintendent's room. I've something to tell you. I learned from Dearborn's widow this afternoon that Dearborn intended to bolt after the accident. I suppose our friend the Superintendent would say that it was delirium, but there was method in his madness. He gave his wife a cheque for £200, quite legibly written, to cover her expenses while he was hunting for a new hiding-place. He didn't put it like that, of course, but that's what he meant."

"But that's very important."

"It is, but it's time to admit that we are up against it. We're not getting on."

"You've still Pengelly to see to-morrow morning."

"I know, but Pengelly, even if he speaks the truth, won't get us any further than the Duke girl did. They say that success in detective work is half chance and the other half the sweat of one's brow, but in this case I want to know when chance is going to take a hand. It's obvious that we shall make no advance until we learn something about Dearborn's past life, and the man who knows most about him—Mr. Todd, the bank manager—can tell us nothing except that he thinks that Dearborn came from London."

"I wonder whether Dearborn was the real name," said Jago. "When a man wishes to hush up his past he's apt to change his name, and he doesn't do it by deed poll either, so that line of country is unpromising. I've got a vague hope that something may turn up when the will is read, but that won't be until to-morrow after the funeral."

"You'll have your work cut out to-morrow, Mr. Richardson," said Jago. "The Superintendent has got a warrant from the magistrates to bring Pengelly down from the quarry early to-morrow morning on a charge of driving a car without a licence and being likely to abscond. I suppose we can do nothing more until then."

After an early breakfast at their hotel, the two metropolitan officers walked to the police station. Superintendent Carstairs met them on the steps.

"Good morning, Mr. Richardson. I have your man in cold storage down below."

"What was his demeanour at the quarry and on the drive down?"

"He didn't say a word."

"Wouldn't you like to be present, Mr. Carstairs? I mean, oughtn't we to interrogate him together?"

The Superintendent shook his head. "That would spoil my record, Mr. Richardson. I want to be able to say that I turned the whole of the inquiry over to you. You had better have him brought up to my office, and I'll post one of my men near the door in case you find that you want him."

Pengelly slouched into the room with a hangdog expression on his face. "Oh, it's you, is it?" he said to Richardson. "I thought I was to be charged with driving without a licence."

"So you will be," said Richardson cheerfully. "I believe you're to be brought up before the Bench to-morrow, but I want to have a straight talk with you on another matter. I can see that you can guess what it is. When I saw you at the quarry yesterday you didn't tell me the whole truth—only part of it. You didn't tell me that you pulled up your lorry farther down the road, and that you hid among the heather to wait for Mr. Dearborn."

"What if I told you that that's a lie?"

"I shouldn't say that if I were in your place, because I have plenty of evidence that you did. I know, for instance, that it wasn't you who stopped Mr. Dearborn's car; that it was someone else who held up the car before it reached you."

Pengelly was a man whose mind worked slowly. He remained silent with his eyes fixed upon his interrogator. Then he asked, "You mean you've found another witness who saw what happened?"

Richardson nodded.

"Well then, if that's so, I don't mind telling you the whole thing."

"You would have done better to tell the whole truth from the start."

"Would I? A man doesn't run his head straight into the noose unless he's a fool. These country police would have fixed the blame on me."

Richardson shook his head.

"Oh, yes, they would. You don't know them as I do."

"Well, let me have your version of what happened."

"What I'm going to tell you isn't my version; it's the truth and nothing but the truth. I did see Dearborn's car waiting at the Duchy Hotel. I knew that if I waited somewhere down the

Sandiland Hill he would be coming along. I stopped the lorry at the roadside after the turn, and walked back until I had a clear view right to the top of the hill. Then the young woman and me squatted down in the heather to wait, and we'd just stowed ourselves out of sight when another chap stepped out into the road between us and the top of the hill."

"What did he look like?"

"Oh, he was an upstanding fellow, but he had his back to me and I couldn't really tell you what he looked like. He was wearing good clothes."

"What happened then?"

"At the moment when he stepped out Dearborn's car came in sight and the fellow in the road stuck out his arms as if he were a railway signal. Dearborn had to pull up whether he liked it or not, otherwise he'd have driven over the chap."

"And then?"

"You must remember that they were a good two hundred yards away, so I couldn't be expected to see all that happened. I remember seeing Dearborn get out of his car with something in his hand—I think it was the starting-handle—and the other fellow went for him with his walking-stick. Dearborn dropped the handle because he'd got a welt on the head from the stick. I think, but I'm not sure, mind, that the stick broke in half with the force of the blow. Anyway, Dearborn was left lying in the road and the other fellow made off into the rough ground. I couldn't see what became of him. I do remember seeing him pick up the starting-handle and the bits of stick and throwing them into the heather before he went."

"And you just left Dearborn lying in the road with a broken head?"

"What else can you expect? It was a frequented road. He was bound to be picked up by someone, but if I'd done it—well, I should have been arrested for murder. No one would have believed me when I said I was giving first aid to the injured."

"I suppose you're ready to put what you've told me into a signed statement?"

"Yes, of course I am, and glad to have got it off my chest. And if you want anybody to corroborate what I've told you, you've only got to go and see Miss Susie Duke in Moorstead. She saw the whole thing."

Sergeant Jago had been taking notes in a combination of short and long-hand system of his own. "I can soon run this off, Mr. Richardson. If you like I'll take it down to the cells and let him sign it there."

"Look here, sir," said Pengelly. "How long are they going to keep me here on this charge of driving without a licence? I only done it because the chap that drives the lorry was down with the 'flu, and if I'm kept hanging about before I'm brought up I shall lose my job at the quarry."

"I hear that you'll be brought up to-morrow, and in any case if you lose your job I'll intercede for you with the foreman. You may be wanted ultimately as a witness of what you've told me."

Pengelly left the room with quite a jaunty step.

Richardson looked at his watch and turned to Jago.

"I'll get you to mind the baby while I'm out. I want to see the people who attend the funeral. When you've written out that statement take it down to the cells and get Pengelly to sign it."

He was not called upon to go as far as the churchyard. The mourners were only two—Mrs. Dearborn and Mr. Todd from the Union Bank. They were about to pass into The Firs as he came up. After greeting them both sympathetically, he asked Mr. Todd whether there was anything in the will so confidential that it would be improper for him to see it.

"Not at all, "was the answer;" in fact I was about to suggest to Mrs. Dearborn that you should be present when I read the will to her."

"Of course I should like you to be present, Mr. Richardson," echoed the widow.

She conducted them into the sitting-room, where without further preface, Mr. Todd drew from his pocket a folded sheet of thick paper, cleared his throat and began to read.

"This is the last will of me, Charles Dearborn, of The Firs, Winterton, in the county of Devon, whereby I revoke all previous wills and testamentary dispositions."

The will was quite short; it left the whole of the estate to the testator's wife, Margaret Dearborn, with the exception of a legacy of one hundred pounds to his executor, William Todd. It ended, "And I hereby appoint the said William Todd sole executor of this my will." It was dated 11th May, 1935.

"That was about the time when the purchase of the quarry was completed," explained Mr. Todd.

"Who witnessed the signature?"

"I called in two of my clerks to witness it."

"Excuse me, Mr. Todd. May I look at the document itself?"

"Certainly. Probably you are not acquainted with the handwriting of the testator, but I can assure you that the writing was his."

"And he brought this to you for the attestation clause, or did he write the will in your office?"

"That was the curious part of the transaction. He asked for a sheet of stout paper, sat down at my table in the bank and dashed off the will without a moment's hesitation. It was, an extraordinary feat in will-making. I told him so at the time and he said that he had a good memory. It struck me that at some time in his career he must have been in a solicitor's office."

Richardson handed back the will. "What you have told me, Mr. Todd, is very interesting. Now, I suppose, you will proceed to prove the will and let this poor lady enjoy her fortune."

"Happily the bank's solicitor will relieve me of all the legal formalities, and we shall be in a position to advance to Mrs. Dearborn all that she may require for current expenses."

Chapter Eight

Richardson left The Firs in deep thought. Quite unconsciously the bank manager had given him what might prove to be a new and most important clue; the dead man had had a legal training in a solicitor's office. But a fraudulent solicitor who had robbed his clients of £35,000 could scarcely have got away with it without being arrested and prosecuted; yet here was this man Dearborn depositing £25,000 in the bank.

Was the man who attacked him on the moor a guilty confederate who had chanced to recognize him? It could not have been a client whom he had robbed; a client would have gone direct to the police as soon as he discovered the hiding-place of the thief. What was to be the next step?

Sergeant Jago was at the door of the police station; he had been with Superintendent Carstairs to the court.

"Pengelly gave no trouble," he said. "He pleaded guilty and they fined him five pounds. He couldn't pay that amount so we brought him back."

"I'm glad of that. I want to see him again. Can you get him up here?"

"I'll see. Mr. Carstairs is away, getting his dinner, but the sub-inspector won't make any difficulty." Five minutes later Pengelly was brought into the office. He was bursting to impart his grievance, but Richardson was too quick for him.

"I've only one question to ask you, Pengelly. What sort of age was the man who attacked Dearborn with a stick—a very young man, not much more than a boy?"

"A boy? Not a bit of it. He seemed to me a man of about Dearborn's age, or even older, as far as I could judge at that distance. But look here, sir, I don't know what these police are up to. I've told them that if they let me go back to the quarry, I can raise the money for my fine, partly from my mates and partly from an advance on my wages. But this Superintendent won't listen to that. The magistrates gave me a month's imprisonment if I didn't pay, and if they shut me up for a month my job will get filled up. I wish you'd have a word with the Superintendent."

"All right, Pengelly, I will."

As soon as he had left the room Jago explained the situation. "Mr. Carstairs is counting upon holding Pengelly until there's sufficient evidence for charging him with wilful murder. That's why he won't let him go back to the quarry to raise the money for his fine."

"It's going to be a ticklish business. Either the Superintendent leaves the case entirely to me, as he said he would, or I'll have to throw up the case because he will keep butting in."

"I'm afraid Mr. Carstairs belongs to that breed of men you find in South Devon who turn mulish if they're not carefully handled. It would be a thousand pities if you chucked the case up just when we seem to be on the point of getting home."

"I've never chucked a case yet and I don't want to start now. I'm going to sit in this chair until Mr. Carstairs has finished his lunch and smoked his pipe, and then I'm going to have it out with him," said Richardson. "But I won't tread on his South Devon toes more than I'm obliged to."

"But you'll get no lunch, Mr. Richardson."

"Oh, never mind about lunch: that can wait." Jago lifted his head to listen. "I think I hear the Superintendent. Shall I tell him you would like to speak to him?"

"Yes, and see that we're not interrupted."

In the Superintendent's expression and bearing there was much that reminded Richardson of a small boy whom he had caught stealing apples from his father's orchard in Scotland. He rose hurriedly from his chair. "Let me give you your own seat, Mr. Carstairs. I hear that Pengelly pleaded guilty this morning and was fined five pounds. I suppose you'll give him time and facilities for finding the money?"

"He'll have all the time he wants," replied Carstairs grimly, "but as for facilities…"

"Are you still of the opinion that he was guilty of the murder?"

"I am."

"That's rather unfortunate, Mr. Carstairs, because I shall want to use him as a principal Crown witness against the real murderer when we have found him."

Carstairs, looking more obstinate than ever, emitted a short laugh.

"You may remember," continued Richardson, "that when I came down here you gave me to understand that I was to have a free hand in investigating this case, and now I find that this is not to be so—that one of the chief obstacles is likely to be yourself. I shall have to reconsider my position."

"What do you mean by that, Mr. Richardson? Haven't I done everything in my power to help you? But you can't expect me to neglect my own duties as Superintendent of this division and let a man who is clearly guilty of murder go free and abscond?"

"This puts me in a very difficult position, Mr. Carstairs. I have already got some way in the case. I have found the writer of the anonymous letters; I have one or two promising clues which

I haven't communicated to you because you gave me to understand that you wished me to take entire responsibility, and now you want to take things out of my hands. I'm really sorry to have to give up the case, but in view of your attitude there seems to be no other course. I must return to London to-night and leave you to carry on."

"Come, come, we don't want to fall out at this stage. You can't shake my opinion that Pengelly is the guilty man, but how can I bring it home to him without your help?"

"Oh, of course before I go I'll leave you copies of all the statements I have taken…"

"Yes, but if you go back and report to your Chiefs that you are throwing up the case because I'm obstructing you, how shall I look when they write to the Chief Constable? I don't want to butt in. You mustn't think that. I want nothing more than to help you. What do you want me to do?"

"I want you to let Pengelly go up to the quarry—in custody, of course, as far as the quarry gates—and to let him get about among his mates and speak to the manager about getting an advance on his wages. Then, if he can raise the money to pay his fine, I want you to let him get back to work. You can make what arrangements you like with the foreman about letting you know if he leaves." The Superintendent's face fell. "I shouldn't be urging you to do this, Mr. Carstairs, if I didn't feel sure that you'll be grateful to me afterwards. Then, if you like to work the case with me, I shall be only too glad."

"Very well, Mr. Richardson, I'll do as you say, but I'd like you to remember when you've cleared up the whole case that my instinct was right from the first. What's the next step you propose to take?"

"I propose to see the manager of the Duchy Hotel in Duketon."

"Then you'll want the car; it shall be ready for you at any hour you name."

Arrived at the Duchy Hotel, Richardson ordered a sandwich and a glass of beer in the bar parlour and asked the waitress to tell the manager that he wished to see him. Scenting sensational gossip, the manager lost no time in obeying the summons. He entered the room on tiptoe and shut the door carefully behind him.

"I thought it must be you. Now, tell me what I can do for you?"

"When I called on you last time, Mr. Tovey, I told you that we were police officers, but I don't think I told you to what police force we belonged. We have come down from Scotland Yard."

The manager purred with satisfaction at being the only man in Duketon who was trusted with so portentous a secret.

Richardson continued: "I want you to cast your memory back to the last evening when Mr. Dearborn had tea at this hotel. Do you, or any members of your staff, remember a stranger being at the hotel that day? It was the 29th September, a Saturday."

The manager shook his head several times before he spoke. "Saturday is one of our char-à-banc days and that means that the whole place is full of strangers, and as a rule there's such a lot of them that you couldn't expect my barmaid or anyone else to remember what any of them looked like."

"I was afraid that it might be so, but let me put another question to you. Do you remember whether any visitor to the hotel spoke to you about Mr. Dearborn?"

The manager perked up. "I do remember an incident that happened this summer about two months ago, though it didn't lead to anything. One of these hikers dressed in shorts—quite a boy, he was—stopped a night in the hotel. He was here just about the time when the char-à-banc turns up, and he was alone in the bar when the people began to come in. Then Mr. Dearborn drove up in his car and came in; the room was pretty full and I suppose it was that that kept him from ordering any refreshment. I remember this because I ran after him to tell him I'd serve him myself, but he wouldn't stop, and as I came back from the door this young hiker boy called me and asked, ' Isn't that Mr.—?'" The landlord scratched his head. "Lord, I've forgotten the name—it wasn't a very common name. I said, 'No, that's Mr. Dearborn.' He said, 'I can't be mistaken. If that isn't Mr.'—whatever the name was—'it's his double. Where does he live?' and I told him, Winterton."

"Did you tell him anything else about Mr. Dearborn?"

"I think I told him he'd bought a quarry; there wasn't much to tell him because I didn't know much, nor did anyone else."

"Did the youth go off in the direction of Winterton?"

"I'm sure I can't tell you which way he went."

"Was there anything peculiar about the boy—anything to distinguish him by?"

"Now you come to speak of it, there was. He was sandy-haired and he'd more freckles on his face than I've ever seen on anyone. I'll bet he was called 'Freckles' at school."

"I don't suppose you'll have the luck to see him again this year, it's getting late for hikers, but if you do I wish you'd ring up the Superintendent of police at Winterton."

"Is he a criminal?" asked the manager with brightening interest.

"Oh no, but I'd like to ask him a few questions. He may be an important witness in a case we have on hand. If by any chance you remember that name you forgot, you'll be sure to let us know. Didn't you make him register as he was stopping the night in the hotel?"

"Well, sir, you know what it is, people coming in and out the whole day long. I can't swear to it that he was made to register, especially as he was a hiker. I hope you're not going to mention this to the Devon police and get me into trouble."

"No," said Richardson with a smile, "the Devon police must look after their own job."

Richardson had left Sergeant Jago in Winterton with instructions to see what happened to Pengelly during his absence. When he returned to the police station Jago came out to meet him.

"Pengelly's still in the cells below," he murmured. "When I asked the Superintendent what time he was going up to the quarry, he said he could do nothing until you came back, because you'd got the car."

"Quite right, but I'll slip in and tell Mr. Carstairs that I shan't want the car again to-day."

He found the Superintendent in his own room, looking through a report from his own sub-divisions.

"You haven't been long, Mr, Richardson," he said. "No, but I've got some quite interesting information by my visit to the Duchy Hotel." He proceeded to describe his interview with the manager, but he noticed that Carstairs was not listening.

"I suppose you still insist on my sending Pengelly up to the quarry?" said the Superintendent.

"It's not a question of insisting. I thought you agreed this morning that that should be done. The car's at the door now."

"All right, then; I'll send him up, and if he pays his fine I suppose we must leave him there."

"Yes, there's no other course possible, if I'm to continue on the case."

Carstairs went heavily out of the room and could be heard giving orders to two of his men. Presently Pengelly passed the door in handcuffs and was taken out to the car. Richardson found Carstairs on the steps, superintending the operation. He led him aside.

"Those cuffs must come off before he gets to the quarry gate," he said with decision. "It'll ruin everything if he goes clanking in with the cuffs on. Surely the sergeant can carry them in his pouch and use them only if the man attempts to bolt."

Very reluctantly, Carstairs gave the desired order; the car drove off.

"Four o'clock," said Richardson, looking at his watch; "I'll get Sergeant Jago to come with me to The Firs, and ask Mrs. Dearborn to allow us to look for any private papers that her husband may have left behind him."

"Certainly, Mr. Richardson, you couldn't do better."

The two officers walked towards The Firs.

"Did you get anything useful out of that manager?" asked Jago.

"It would have been useful if he hadn't got a memory like a sieve." Richardson related the incident. "If he could have remembered that name I should feel that we were within a measurable distance of clearing up the case, but when a man forgets, and then says that it wasn't quite a common name, and you suggest various names to him, you are asking for trouble. You know the kind of thing, 'Smith? Jones? Johnson? Wilson? Clark?' Ten to one he'll say it was Wilson, to the best of his belief, and then, when you've found your man and he answers to the name of Carter, your witness will say cheerfully, 'Yes, how stupid of me, confusing Wilson and Carter.' For all the use that publican is likely to be in the matter of names, I might just as well not have seen him."

"But that hiker was freckled. Didn't the naval officer talk about a youth with freckles?"

"He did, and I shouldn't be surprised to find that both of them were referring to the same fellow. Unfortunately, we can't sit down and twiddle our thumbs until a youth with freckles chooses to take pity on us."

They had reached The Firs. As usual at this particular hour, Mrs. Dearborn was in her garden. She had come to look upon Richardson as a personal friend, and she hurried forward to welcome him.

"I'm sorry to trouble you again, Mrs. Dearborn, but we have now definite information that your husband was attacked by a stranger. It is more important than ever that we should know something about his past life—that is, where he came from. Can we look through his papers?"

"I'm afraid you won't find any; I've already been through all the drawers and cupboards which my husband used, and I've gone through the papers in his desk. There were only three or four receipted bills and a sort of balance-sheet of his quarry. It was most disappointing, but here are his keys and I suggest that you do your own searching."

The searching did not take long. As Mrs. Dearborn had said, there were practically no private papers except a bank pass-book and the quarry accounts. With her help they looked through the dead man's clothes, searching for any name or mark that might give them a clue, but they found none—nothing that would throw any light upon Dearborn's past life. When the officers took their leave they made for the railway station and inquired from the man who clipped the tickets whether he remembered a youth abundantly freckled passing the barrier on Sunday.

"Freckled, you say? What sort of age was he?"

"Oh, eighteen or nineteen, I should say."

The railway porter and the lamp man had drifted up to listen to the conversation.

"I remember the chap," said the porter. "Don't you remember," he added to the ticket-collector; "don't you remember me asking you if you'd ever seen freckles like that before? There were more freckles than skin on his face. He went by the afternoon train to North Road."

"I remember the chap now," said the ticket man. "He had a return third to Paddington."

Chapter Nine

As they walked back from the railway station Richardson was in the depths of gloom. "To search London for a sandy-haired young man with freckles—and that's all we have to go upon—would be sheer lunacy."

"Couldn't you advertise?" asked Jago hopefully.

"What, and call attention to a physical defect as an inducement for a youth to come forward? Probably he spends every spare shilling in buying lotions for the face."

"But the people who laugh at his freckles might answer the advertisement."

"Some hundreds of them would, in the hope of getting a free trip down into Devonshire, but think of the expense. What would the Receiver of the Metropolitan Police say about it?"

"Where are we going to now?" asked Jago, giving up the attempt to lift the clouds from his chief's face.

"To the police station, I suppose," said Richardson wearily.

The station sergeant was standing on the steps, gazing down the road; he disappeared as soon as he saw them, apparently to report their arrival to the Superintendent, for Carstairs himself lumbered out on to the threshold.

"You're wanted on the telephone, Mr. Richardson—badly wanted, I judge, by the tone of the speaker."

"Did he give his name?"

"He did. He said he was Lieutenant Cosway; he's holding the line now."

Richardson hurried to the instrument. "Is that you, Mr. Cosway? Chief Inspector Richardson speaking."

"Praise be to God! I've got you at last. Come as quick as you can to The Firs and I'll start right away from here and meet you half-way, to tell you what it's all about. You'll hear something to your advantage."

Richardson stopped only to tell Sergeant Jago to stand by until the car returned from the quarry and then to follow him to The Firs with the news whether Pengelly had paid his fine or not. Then he hurried off. He could walk fast but the naval lieutenant could walk faster still; he met him at less than halfway.

"Be prepared for a shock, Mr. Richardson," he said. "You're going to meet what I've never seen before—the publicity agent of a film star, straight out of Hollywood. Probably you know the breed. If he came on board my ship I should chuck him into the sea without referring to the captain in the hope that he couldn't swim."

"Where is he?"

"Closeted with that poor widow in The Firs. She's looking round helplessly for a dictionary of Hollywood American. When I left her she had grasped the startling fact that his client is the first Mrs. Dearborn."

"Good God!"

"You have used the exact words that came to my lips when I saw the gentleman. I'll tell you how it all happened. My mother wished to be kind to the poor widow and sent me down to ask if she might call. I found Mrs. Dearborn in the garden, and while we were fixing things up a monstrous Rolls Royce pulled up at the gate, and out of it rolled a thing in a fur coat with a cigar dangling from the corner of his mouth. He came towards us and asked, 'Say, are you Mrs. Dearborn? Well, I've come down to break some bad news to you gently. The first Mrs. Dearborn is still alive. You'll have seen her on the screen many times in your sweet life—Jane Smith, that's her. A stunt of mine to give her a plain name—we've had too many high-falutin' ones. I'm her publicity agent.'"

"How did Mrs. Dearborn take it?"

"Oh, she was very calm. She asked the animal to come into the house, and told me to ring you up and get you to come round to deal with him. If he hasn't eaten her, we shall find them in the sitting-room. I suppose with your vast experience you'll know how to handle the situation."

They had reached the gate. Mrs. Dearborn had left the sitting-room; she was at the front door.

"Where is he?" asked Cosway. She pointed mutely to the room behind her. "Come along," said Cosway, "we'll tackle him together."

Cosway had not exaggerated the appearance of the visitor; blatancy oozed out of him—it was, after all, his bread and butter. Cosway introduced Richardson as Mrs. Dearborn's legal adviser.

"Ah! Then you're just the guy I need. I've come down to get the death certificate of the late Dearborn and I guess you can supply the goods. I tell you, boy, this is going to be the finest publicity stunt Jane's ever had. I haven't brought the cameraman with me to-day, but I'll have them all here tomorrow and you'll all be in it. Even you, sir, a naval officer and all. You can stick on your uniform tomorrow—I don't mind the expense of shooting you once—and then we'll have the death certificate ten times life-size, and, of course, the second Mrs. Dearborn in her widow's weeds. Say, but it's going to be a cinch!"

"This is the moment for that half walking-stick," murmured Cosway. "Have you got it handy?"

Richardson took a note-book from his pocket and as soon as the publicity agent stopped for breath he said, "May I ask you a few questions, and will you make the answers as short as possible? When did this lady whom you call Jane Smith marry Mr. Dearborn?"

"I haven't got the date with me, but I bet she has."

"Where did the marriage take place?"

"I can't tell you that either, but she'd know."

"Have you a photograph of the man she married?"

"Not with me, I haven't."

"But she has?"

"Sure."

"May I have your business card?"

"Sure you may." The publicity agent lugged out of his pocket a packet of cards of outsize and Richardson read, "Mr. Franklyn Jute."

"And now you have my card I'll ask you to deliver the goods. The certificate of death is what I need. I'm willing to pay for it, but have it I must if I'm to get back to London to-night."

Richardson assumed an expression of judicial severity which he was far from feeling. "You come down here, sir, with an unsupported statement, without a tittle of evidence, and expect us to give you copies of official documents. You'll get nothing of the kind until the lady you represent produces her proofs. She must come here herself."

"She can't do that. She's rehearsing at Twickenham for this new film of hers."

"Very well, then, if you'll give me her address, I'll go up and see her."

"She has an apartment—number 21 Arcadia Mansions."

"Good. Then I'll be up to-morrow."

"I warn you that she doesn't hand out interviews as easy as that. She's rehearsing all day."

"Except on Sunday," corrected Richardson. "I'm in no hurry; I can wait until Sunday, but if you want to get on with it perhaps you can arrange for her to see me to-morrow afternoon at five o'clock."

"Wall I knew this country was slow before I crossed the pond, but I didn't know it was as slow as this. It means I've had all this journey for nothing, and it puts off the publicity stunt that I was banking on."

"Because you didn't bring your proofs with you."

"Wal now, if I'm beat I'm beat and that's all there is to it. But remember this, not a word to any of the folks down here. I don't give over my best stuff in dribs and drabs. All or none is my motto—all or nothing, that's me. I guess it'll be waste of time for me to hang around if I'm not to get any more without what you call proofs. It's a disease you all have over here and that's why you can't get on. Lord! In my country a guy that wants proofs before he'll get a move on would go under. I'll be getting back to the Savoy—that's my perch in slow old London—and I'll ring up Jane and get her to hand out an interview with you at five o'clock to-morrow. You come around to the Savoy Hotel at four to-morrow and I'll take you to her. So long!"

They heard the Rolls Royce begin to purr in the road outside, and at the same moment Sergeant Jago knocked at the door. Richardson went out to him.

"Pengelly has paid his fine," said Jago in a hoarse whisper.

"So that's that," said Richardson; "and now we need another starting-point."

"Won't this come to anything?"

"I can't say yet, but I mean to catch the next train to London."

"And what about me?"

"You'll stay here to keep in touch with the County Police until I return or send you a wire to recall you."

"What's in the wind?"

"Another woman who claims to be Mrs. Dearborn. I'm going up to inspect her proofs."

Richardson returned to the sitting-room. "Have you a photograph of your late husband?" he asked.

"No, he had a prejudice against being photographed, but if you would let me come up to London with you, and the other lady who claims to be Mrs. Dearborn has a portrait, I could tell you at once whether it was my husband."

"Are you sure it wouldn't be a shock to you?" asked Richardson.

"It would be far better for me than to stay down here without knowing what was going on."

Cosway intervened. "You couldn't do better than take her with you, Mr. Richardson. She may be able to clear up the whole mystery. Besides, you will both see what a film star looks like when she's gone into a publicity agent as a little boy goes into trousers. If I could keep my hands off the gentleman who has just left us I'd come myself."

"I won't travel up with you this evening, Mr. Richardson," said Mrs. Dearborn, "because I can easily get to the Savoy Hotel by four o'clock by taking an early morning train. In the meantime I'll spend the evening in collecting specimens of my husband's handwriting and signature, and any other particulars that may be useful. When I get to London I will take a taxi to the Savoy and ask for Mr. Franklyn Jute."

"I won't hear of that, Mrs. Dearborn. I'll meet you at Waterloo and take you to the hotel. Goodbye till to-morrow."

Sergeant Jago walked with his chief to their hotel, discussing the case with him as they went. "I confess I don't see how it's to help us much, even if you do find that Dearborn had another wife living before he married that poor lady," said the sergeant.

"It won't help us at all except as a starting-point. At present we have nothing whatever to work upon, but if this film star was really married to the fellow she will be able to tell us a lot about his past life. Dearborn is an uncommon name. If it were assumed, where did he get it from? The fact is, anything may turn out to be a starting-point."

"Will you go to C.O. to-morrow morning?" asked Jago, using the familiar abbreviation for the Central Office.

"Yes, that's one of my reasons for going. I want to see how the case strikes the Superintendent and Mr. Morden." Richardson looked at his watch. "We've not too much time if I'm to catch that train at Tavistock. Will you run into the police station and see whether you can wheedle the car out of Mr. Carstairs while I go on to get my bag?"

"Right you are. I'll bring the car round to the hotel and come down with you to the station." Richardson caught the train by the skin of his teeth, and reached Waterloo in the early hours of the morning. He put up at the Charing Cross Hotel, and at nine o'clock the next morning he was discussing the case with Superintendent Witchard of the C.I.D. His greeting was not encouraging.

"I was talking about your case with Mr. Morden only this morning," he said. "You don't seem to be getting on."

"Quite true, Mr. Witchard. We have cleared up the question of the anonymous letters, but as you have seen from my reports, we are now up against a dead wall. I suppose that you want me back?"

"I don't see much object in trying to convert an ordinary motor accident into a murder. After all, you have the jury's verdict at the inquest—death as the result of a motor accident. There are hundreds of such cases every year. Besides, there's a mass of work accumulating, and with a Chief Inspector short I don't know how we're going to cope with it. But you had better see Mr. Morden and hear what he has got to say."

Witchard rang a bell and told the messenger to let him know as soon as the Assistant Commissioner came in.

"Mr. Morden has just come in, sir."

"Then come along, Richardson. We'll go in now before he has time to tackle one of the new cases on the table. Stop here," he added when they reached the door; "I'll call you in presently."

He found Morden just sitting down to his morning's work. "I've Chief Inspector Richardson waiting outside, sir," he said. "He's come up to London in connection with that Devon case. I thought you might like to see him."

"Quite right. Call him in."

The Superintendent opened the door and stood aside to allow Richardson to approach the table.

Morden adjusted his glasses. "What has brought you to London, Mr. Richardson? Can't you get on with the case?"

Richardson explained the object of his visit. Morden smiled. "You've done a good deal in clearing up the anonymous letters," he said.

"I've had luck, sir, in that, but I can't get a starting-point for clearing up Dearborn's identity."

"Unless you find that this film star was his first wife, you mean?"

"Yes, sir."

"Mr. Witchard suggested that with the coroner's verdict, attributing death to a motor accident, we might leave it at that. Are you yourself convinced that it was a case of murder?"

"Yes, sir, I am, and so are the Devon police. We have two eye-witnesses of the attack, besides the actual weapon used, and a medical certificate that death was probably due to an assault."

"I see. You think that the coroner's verdict can be ignored in view of fresh evidence. In a case like this I fancy that you are right. At any rate one thing is clear: you must go on with the case until you've solved it. Don't you agree, Mr. Witchard?"

"Yes, sir, I suppose so."

"Are you going to see that woman this afternoon?"

"Yes, sir."

"Well, let me know the result before you go back. Even if it all comes to nothing we can't afford to throw up the case at this stage. Besides, if it is any comfort to you, let me tell you that when a case seems really hopeless, that is the moment when luck usually steps in to take a hand in the game."

"Very good, sir—if Mr. Witchard can spare me for a few days longer…I'll send in a report before I leave town."

"When are you going back?"

"By to-night's train, if I can get done in time."

It must be confessed that there was satisfaction among the seniors of the Central Office when they learned that their junior colleague was not making headway with his case in Devonshire. "That's the worst of promoting men out of their turn," said one of them. "I could have done with a little holiday in South Devon myself."

But Richardson, with his chief's encouragement still ringing in his ears, left Scotland Yard with a springy step, reflecting that the darkest hour comes always just before dawn. There was always the chance that he might meet the boy with the freckles. He found himself scanning the features of every lad he passed in the street. All the light-haired lads seemed to have more than their share of freckles, and he reflected that lads of that age in a population of eight millions must run into several hundred thousand.

Chapter Ten

IN THE EARLY afternoon of the same day, Richardson took his stand at the gate where the tickets are collected in Waterloo station. When the first batch of people in a hurry had come through and the more leisurely were strung out behind them, he saw Mrs. Dearborn hurrying towards him. Her eyesight was good; she had recognized him from a considerable distance; she was smiling.

"It gives one confidence to find a friend waiting for one," was her greeting as she shook hands.

"What have you brought with you, Mrs. Dearborn?"

"I couldn't find much to bring. My marriage certificate, of course, and the last cheque my husband gave me, which bears his signature. I haven't cashed it yet, and it is more clearly written than any other of his signatures that I found in the house."

"I'm afraid that the marriage certificate won't be of much use to us this afternoon. Were you married in the church at Winterton?"

"No, we were married in the registry office in Plymouth."

"Then the certificate will only be a copy of the register, and the handwriting is probably that of the registrar or his clerk."

"Besides the certificate and cheque, I've brought you this slip of paper on which I've marked the sizes of my late husband's collars, shoes and gloves; I thought they might come in useful."

"I think they may," said Richardson, folding the paper and storing it away in his pocket-book. "And now we ought to be moving towards the Savoy Hotel. That publicity man made an appointment for us at four o'clock and it's already past the hour. We must take a taxi."

On arriving at the hotel they were told that they would find Mr. Jute waiting for them in the lounge. A page was sent to call him.

He came hurrying out, bursting with news. "See here, now, I've fixed up your interview with Jane for five o'clock and she's a busy woman. I'll tell you it was some job to fix it, but I don't take no for an answer. What I say goes with her."

He appeared to notice Mrs. Dearborn for the first time. "So you've come up too, madam. Lord! What couldn't we do with the photographer at this interview. 'The two Mrs. Dearborns, past and present.' Say, a notion like that should be acted on quick!

We'll stop on the way for a camera-man and take him along with us. Jane will be all for it. You needn't worry about her."

Richardson checked him. "We'll do nothing of the kind, Mr. Jute. You told me yesterday that your plan was to get all your proofs complete before you ventured into publicity, and I don't think that anything will be cleared up to-day."

"Say! But isn't that the lawyer every time," said Jute, appealing to Mrs. Dearborn. "Always put off till to-morrow what you can do to-day. Well then, we'll leave out the camera-man and let the two ladies fight it out between them. I'll back Jane every time to get home with the goods. It's all got to be cleared up this afternoon because nothing will keep her in London on a Sunday. She's a riverside home to go to."

The hotel porter signalled to a taxi; the publicity agent gave the address, "Arcadia Mansions, Regent's Park." During the drive Richardson had an opportunity for studying the demeanour of Mrs. Dearborn. She was perfectly calm and collected, even the unwelcome presence of Mr. Franklyn Jute seemed undisturbing to her; there was no sign of anxiety about the coming interview which might affect her status. He began to admire her strength of character more than ever.

Arcadia Mansions was a rabbit warren of flats of all sizes from the costly to the modest. Mr. Jute knew his way about them. Leaving Richardson to pay the taxi he conducted Mrs. Dearborn to the gates of the lift and pushed the switch. A liftboy slid silently down with his conveyance, and when Richardson had joined them the three were whisked up to the third floor and were directed to turn to the left for number twenty-one.

"Don't you worry, sonny, I knew the way to this apartment when you were still sucking a bottle in your cradle."

A touch on the bell brought a neatly attired maid to the flat door. She appeared to recognize Mr. Franklyn Jute, for her manner stiffened; apparently she had suffered from his jocularity on former occasions.

"You'll tell Miss Jane Smith that three visitors are waiting to see her, and that the sooner she comes the sooner they'll go."

"What name shall I give?"

"Why, you know mine; that'll be enough. The other two are going to be a surprise to her."

"She won't be a minute."

"Yes, but I know what only a minute means with Miss Jane Smith. Give her a hint to drop the lipstick and walk right in."

The maid tossed her head and withdrew.

"You'd better make yourselves at home," said Mr. Jute, indicating the extremely modern-looking chairs dotted about the room.

For once Miss Jane Smith, otherwise Mrs. Dearborn, played no tricks with the time; she came bustling in. Richardson rose. She was a young woman with an assured manner and with what would pass for striking good looks when represented on the screen. She took in her visitors at a glance. The introductions were made by her publicity agent.

"This is the other Mrs. Dearborn and that gentleman over there is her lawyer. So now you know where you are."

The lady smiled broadly, displaying a very perfect set of teeth, and begged the three to be seated. "I shan't have to detain you long," she said. "I have the paper here—my marriage certificate. As you'll see, I was married to Charles Dearborn eight years ago at St. Matthew's Church, Abbott's Ashton, Bristol. My people lived there; so did his."

"How long were you together?" asked Richardson.

She laughed shortly. "I thought one of you would ask that. It was just under two years when he took his hat and walked out on me. No reason given—just took his hat."

"Incompatibility of temper?" Suggested Richardson gently.

"I guess if it was, the temper was all on my side. He was a poor, snivelling kind of man, always wanting to get into a corner with some book or other when I wanted him to be up and doing something for a living. Well, we needn't waste time over him. If he's dead, as I hope he is, because that kind of man is sure to be in heaven, all I want is a certificate of his death which will leave me free to marry again."

"I see," said Richardson, returning the marriage certificate, "that he had the same first name as this lady's husband. You have your marriage certificate with you, Mrs. Dearborn; you might show it to this lady."

Jane Smith examined it. "That's all right; it's the same man. Married again three years ago when I was in Hollywood—just the sort of thing he would do—said nothing to you about having been married before?" Mrs. Dearborn shook her head. "I guessed as much." She turned to Richardson. "All I want from you is a copy of his death certificate and then we can get on."

"I think I ought to tell you," said Richardson, "that this lady's husband left a good bit of money behind him."

For the first time the lady's confidence seemed to wilt. "Gee! That wasn't like my Charles."

"He may have won the money in the Irish Sweepstake," observed Mr. Franklyn Jute.

"He wouldn't have known enough to buy a ticket," said the lady scornfully.

"We hoped that you might have a photograph and letters of your husband's."

"Then your hopes let you down badly," she retorted. "There were photographs and letters, but I remember tearing them all up and putting the pieces on the fire in his presence the day before he walked out on me."

"Would you recognize his signature if you saw it?"

"I might."

"Well, here's a specimen." Richardson showed her Mrs. Dearborn's cheque for £200.

She looked keenly at the signature. "That's his right enough, but I see that he'd started disguising it. That was to keep me from claiming any of the money—just the kind of dirty trick he'd have done." She turned to the other woman. "You needn't worry about the money, dearie; I make all I need by my work. All I want is that death certificate to know that I'm free to marry again. You see, it helps a girl to be married to the manager of the studio she's working in, and that's my case."

"Do you happen to know the sizes of your husband's collars and boots and gloves?"

"Not at this distance of time I don't, but I can tell you what he looked like. He was just the ordinary size of a man, with dark brown hair, a pale, thin face, clean-shaven, and a let-me-get-out-of-your-way style of walking."

"This lady's husband wore a moustache."

"That don't surprise me; he grew it, of course, as a disguise for fear that one day I'd meet him in the street and take him home with me. You see, he was addicted to reading these detective yarns, so he'd get plenty of ideas for disguising himself."

Mr. Jute, who had never been condemned to so long a period of silence before, turned to Mrs. Dearborn. "How does that description kind of fit your husband? It seems pretty good to me."

"It's a description that would fit half the men you meet on the London streets," said Richardson; "we should want something better than that."

"I don't see what we're all running round in circles about," said the film star. "It isn't money that I'm after. Dearborn isn't a common name and when you get Charles attached to it, belonging to a man who keeps his past to himself, what other proof do you want? If I had a death certificate of your man I could marry again right away and no questions asked. It's not going to cost you a cent, I'll pay all the expenses, and if it's publicity you're afraid of, I'll soon stop that, won't I, Franklyn?"

Mr. Jute appeared pained. "I'm the man who calls the tune in the publicity music," he reminded her.

"I know, but I'm the girl who can dig her toes in if she doesn't get what she wants, and you can put that in your pipe and smoke it."

It was evident that Mr. Franklyn Jute had to suffer sometimes from the shortness of his client's temper. Richardson hastened to create a diversion. "If you don't mind, I should like to ask whether your husband's relations are still living in Abbott's Ashton?"

"Oh, yes, they're there all right, but you won't get a word out of them. I've tried myself, and all they say is that they haven't heard from him for six years and they don't know whether he's alive or dead."

"Don't you think that when your husband's relations read of his death in the paper as you did yourself, they would have come down to make inquiries, or at any rate sent someone down?"

Jane Smith looked perturbed, and turning to the widow asked, "Didn't anyone call on you?"

"I didn't see anyone myself, but a neighbour told me that a young man came down and asked where my husband was living." She turned to Richardson. "Didn't Mr. Cosway tell you about that young man with freckles?"

"Freckles!" screamed Jane, with real triumph in her voice. "Why, that was his young brother, Albert. He'd more freckles on his face than skin."

"There you are!" exclaimed Jute. "Now you've got your proof and I'll thank you for that death certificate. We can have a camera-man down here when you hand it to Jane."

Richardson laughed. "We haven't yet got to that point, Mr. Jute. To-day is Saturday. I shall go down to Bristol to-night and visit Mr. Dearborn's family."

"But to-morrow's Sunday," objected Jane; "you're sure not going to work on Sunday."

"Sunday's a good day for finding people at home."

"Now see here, sir," interrupted Mr. Jute; "publicity don't matter to you folks in the law, but to us in the picture world it's everything. I've had enough of these delays. What's to stop me writing a paragraph, 'Freckled boy becomes key to mystery of fate of Jane Smith's husband. Surprising developments. Lawyers beside themselves,' and starting work with that? Then we'll have a picture of the boy with freckles touched up, and an interview with him about his dead brother. We'll make him have attended the funeral. What's wrong with that for a send-off—with other startling details to follow?"

Speaking in a quiet voice Richardson asked, "And what is to happen if your startling details turn out to be all wrong and we find that the lady's husband is still alive?"

"Well, we'll have no publicity about it."

"Don't go so fast, Franklyn," said Jane. "You don't want to step into it up to the neck. How would you look if that guy Gover Schoost, who's running the publicity for Dora Spencer, got a hold of it and held you up as a darned liar on both sides of the herring-pond? How d'you look then?"

The publicity agent wilted, as he always did under the lash of Jane Smith's tongue.

Richardson seized the opportunity of his silence to rise and make a signal to Mrs. Dearborn. "Very well, then," he said. "That's arranged, madam?"

"Seems to me you did most of the fixing," replied Jane; "and I don't know now what we've fixed."

"That I go down to Bristol to-night and call on your husband's family to-morrow. They may tell me what they wouldn't tell you."

"And you'll let me know. Come and see me again on Monday at the same time?"

"I can't quite promise that I'll come and see you, but I'll let you know what they say."

Jane's parting words to Mrs. Dearborn were, "Don't you worry about that money he left you, dearie. Nobody's going to take it from you."

Richardson paused on his way out. "There are two small points that I should like to have cleared up, Miss Smith. The first is, what was your husband's profession?"

"The same as his father's. He worked in the same big drapery store in Bristol where his father was the walker. His father got him the job as cashier, but after we married he had words with the boss and he threw him out. After that he did nothing; his plan of life was to live on me, and when I rubbed it in a bit at home he took his hat. What was your other point?"

"Only the address of your husband's parents?"

"Oh, Abbott's Ashton is only a little bit of a place. Everybody knows where they live; it's a red brick villa called Chatsworth. But I doubt whether you'll get anything out of them."

Out in the street Richardson hailed a passing taxi.

"You won't go back to Devonshire to-night, of course. Would you like me to choose an hotel for you?"

"Thank you; I'll go to the Treherne Hotel in Cromwell Road; I've stayed there before."

"I'll come with you, because I'd like to learn your impressions about our recent interview."

He followed her into the car, after giving the address. "Now," he said, "tell me what you thought."

"Well, I was listening closely to all of you. I should think that Miss Jane Smith had always been a very difficult person to live with, and that would be enough to account for her husband leaving her. She said that he was a very quiet, retiring man. So was my husband. When he asked me to marry him he told me frankly that I had a soothing effect upon his nerves, and that he had learned with me what real tranquillity was."

"So we'll call that a point of resemblance," said Richardson.

"Yes, but on the other hand I gathered from that lady that her husband was a poor sort of creature quite incapable of making money. My husband, I should say, was quite the reverse. He was a good man of business, as his bank manager must have told you."

"Have you any other point?"

"Just one—a very small one. The lady said that her husband read detective novels. I never saw mine read anything but his newspaper, but yesterday, when I was putting away some of his clothes, I found two detective stories in his bedroom cupboard."

"Well," said Richardson, "we don't seem to be getting much nearer. When I was examining the two marriage certificates this afternoon I noticed that the age given of the two men corresponded pretty closely, though not the dates of birth."

The taxi pulled up at the Treherne Hotel. Mrs. Dearborn ran up the steps with her small suit-case, leaving Richardson to pay the driver. He found her waiting for him in the hall.

"I still have one thing to tell you, Mr. Richardson. Why shouldn't we have tea together here; it's very quiet."

Richardson looked at his watch. "I mustn't risk missing my train. No; it's all right."

She gave the order and they went into the dining-room to await their tea.

"What I want to tell you is this," she said. "As you know, my husband never talked to me about his past life, and yet on one occasion he did tell me that he had no relations living. He told me this quite spontaneously and that makes me think it may have been true, for if not he would just have maintained silence as he did about everything else in his past life."

"I think that's a very good point, Mrs. Dearborn."

At this moment a waiter entered with their tea, and their conversation was interrupted.

When they were alone again, Richardson took out his pocket-book and laid Mrs. Dearborn's cheque on the table. "I want you to trust me with this cheque until we meet again. I'm going to get a photograph of the marriage register at Abbott's Ashton and the signature on this cheque brought up to the same size, and then get an expert opinion on the handwriting." He gulped down his tea. "And now I fear that I must really take my leave."

"When shall I see you again?" she asked.

"Probably on Monday at Winterton."

Chapter Eleven

BEING LEFT to himself for the week-end was a depressing prospect for Sergeant Jago. He lay awake on the Friday evening wondering how he could usefully spend the two days that were to intervene before his chief's return from London, and before he closed his eyes he had evolved a plan of action that would be highly commended by his chief inspector if it succeeded and could do no harm if it failed. He argued to himself that the man who killed Dearborn had plunged into the bogs on the south side of North Hessary Tor, where there might be tracks made by the half-wild moorland ponies, but no trodden road in the direction of Plymouth until one struck the main road from Tavistock to Winterton; that in the hollow below the Tor there were bogs impassable even to the ponies, and full of traps for the unwary unacquainted with the moor. The murderer, whoever he was, would naturally avoid any public road; the pony tracks he was following came to an end long before they reached the soft bog; having broken his stout walking-stick, he would have nothing in his hand for testing the solidity of the ground that lay before him, and he might well have had to jump from tussock to tussock until with the failing light he plunged into a quaking morass and was bogged.

Jago had a friend in the police force, a Tavistock lad like himself; acting on his advice he might gain the ear of the Chief Constable and have a search made of the hotels and boarding-houses for some visitor who had been "bogged" on the moor, and had had to have his clothes and boots washed and brushed before he could show himself in the streets. It might all come to nothing, but it was worth trying.

Directly after breakfast Jago took the train to Plymouth and found on inquiry at the police station that his friend, Ned Halliday, was booked as a reserve constable that day. This was fortunate because, while he could not engage a man on point duty in conversation for perhaps a quarter of an hour, he could obtain a long interview with him in a corner of the reserve constables' room. It was there that he found him, five minutes after the arrival of the train.

"Good Lord!" exclaimed Halliday, when he saw Jago, "I thought you were catching burglars in London. What are you doing down here?"

"At the moment I'm trying to catch a murderer, by request of the County Chief Constable."

"What! Are you on this Dearborn case that all the papers are full of?"

"I am."

"They might have sent down a better man," said Halliday, guarding himself against the punch in the ribs that he knew was coming.

"Can't you ever be serious for a moment?" inquired Jago. "Not even if I give you a chance of working your promotion?"

"Now you're talking. I could do with a bit of promotion with the pay attached to it."

"Well, look here. The murderer we're looking for ran down the south side of North Hessary Tor, and you know what the bogs are like on that side."

"I don't know, but I can imagine."

"I do know because I've been there. Now this blighter broke his stick over the head of the man he murdered, and to run down at dusk into those bogs without a stick is asking for it."

"You think he's there still with the mud up to his chin?"

"He may be, and it'll save a lot of expense to the Crown if he is, but murderers are not as a rule so easily disposed of, and that's why I've come to you. Couldn't you move your Chief Constable into handing out what we call in London an All Station message, inquiring at every hotel and lodging-house for a man who came in with mud and slime all over his boots and clothes and asked to have them cleaned, on September 29, a Saturday? There can't have been more than one man in Plymouth to have got himself into such a mess. If they run across his tracks, we'd like to know what became of him afterwards."

Halliday considered for a moment. "It could be done, of course. I'm only thinking what would be the best way of getting a move on. I suppose you're not working alone on this case?"

"No; Chief Inspector Richardson is in charge of it."

"Well, wouldn't he be the man to see my chief and make a formal request?"

"He would if he were here, but he's shot off an inquiry in London and he won't be back for a day or two."

"I'll tell you what I can do—see my Inspector and tell him that you want to see the Chief on a very confidential matter connected with the Dearborn murder. That'll make him sit up and take notice, and you can tell him exactly what you want. Sit tight while I dig out Inspector Piggott."

Halliday did not return alone; he brought the Inspector with him. Sergeant Jago stood to attention.

"You want to have a word with the Chief Constable, I understand. Tell me what it's about and I will see whether it can be arranged."

"It's about the man concerned in that Dearborn murder case, Inspector."

"And have you been sent down by the Yard?"

"Yes; I'm assisting Chief Inspector Richardson."

"Come along then; I dare say the Chief would be glad to hear how you're getting on."

They went upstairs; the Inspector knocked at the Chief Constable's door and was called in. He came back and beckoned to Jago, who went into the sanctum and shut the door behind him. At the desk in the middle of the room sat a slim, well-groomed man, who seemed young for the duties imposed upon him. He opened the business at once.

"You are one of the officers engaged in that murder case up on the moor?"

"Yes, sir; Sergeant Jago."

"And you think that the murderer escaped into the rough ground on the south side of North Hessary Tor?"

"Yes, sir; we have two witnesses to prove it."

"Then what do you want me to do?"

"We think that the man was probably a Londoner, or at any rate that he intended to make his way to London. There is every probability that in the dusk he may have got bogged in the rough ground at the bottom of the Tor. He had broken his stick over the head of the man he killed, and if he didn't have a stick and got bogged he must have been in a terrible mess. I was wondering whether it would be possible for you, sir, to have inquiries made around hotels and boarding-houses for information about a man who gave a suit of clothes and a pair of boots to be cleaned on Saturday, the 29th September."

The Chief Constable drummed on the table with his fingers, thinking. "If we did find there had been such a man in Plymouth it doesn't seem to me that it can help you very much."

"It would, sir, if it resulted in our getting a description of him and how he left—whether by train or car."

"Well, I'll see what can be done. If you like to call here to-morrow morning I'll let you know the result."

"As time is of importance," said Jago, "I wonder if you would mind telephoning to the Winterton police station if anything is found out this afternoon. I would then come down and see the people myself, sir."

"Certainly. That shall be done, Sergeant."

Nothing appeared to have been happening in Winterton when Jago reached the police station, but while he was tidying up his notes of the case the reserve constable who kept his ear on the station telephone, put his head in at the door and said, "A trunk call for you, Sergeant."

Jago hurried to the instrument and recognized the voice of his chief. "Is that you, Sergeant Jago? Chief Inspector Richardson speaking. I've been to C.O., and Mr. Morden wants us to carry on."

"Have you had any luck, sir?"

"I can't tell yet, but I've that interview for this afternoon. I'm ringing you up to say that I hope to be back to-morrow morning. I suppose you are tired of kicking your heels with nothing to do."

"I've not been entirely idle, sir. I'm carrying out a little inquiry in Plymouth which may possibly lead to something. It's too long to tell you over the 'phone."

"Good, but you must be careful not to queer our pitch. If you want me you must ring C.O. and I'll get the message. Good-bye."

Lunch-time was approaching; Jago walked down to the hotel, leaving a message with the telephone man to take down in writing any message that might come through for him during his absence. He felt a strange confidence in the promise of the Chief Constable in Plymouth.

On his return to Winterton he learned that a message had been received from the police at Plymouth, telling him to ring them up when he got back from lunch. When he had established the connection a strange voice informed him that it would be well if Sergeant Jago were to report himself at police headquarters as soon as possible.

"Is that in connection with my interview with the Chief Constable this morning?"

"Yes," replied the voice. "We have something to tell you that may be of interest."

Jago decided that he had no right to strain Mr. Carstairs' kindness by asking for the loan of the police car. He glanced at the station clock and found that if he was quick he might catch the 1.17 train to Millbay station. He set out at once. From Millbay station he covered the ground to the Town Hall almost at a run. On giving his name to the reserve officer on duty he was shown into the Inspector's room.

"Sergeant Jago from the Yard? I've a message for you in connection with that inquiry you asked to have carried out this morning. It was quick work. We got the information you wanted within the first half-hour. Here it is." He caught up a slip of flimsy paper. "On 29th September a man staying at the Globe Hotel came in very late when no one was left on duty but the night-porter. His clothing and boots were in a terrible state. He said that he had been bogged on Dartmoor, and that as this was the only suit of clothes he had with him, would the porter clean and brush them and do the same for his shoes. The night-porter will be sent for if desired by the police."

"Where is the Globe Hotel, Inspector? I never heard of it."

"It's not one of the first-class hotels; it's in Emmett Street."

"Thank you. I'll go down there at once."

"Will you want any of us to go with you?"

"Just as you like, Inspector. If you're shorthanded I think I could make the inquiry by myself."

"We're always short-handed here. You'll find the people at the Globe very obliging."

The Globe was certainly not one of the smart hotels of the town, and a man who had been bogged on Dartmoor must have been thankful that it was not. As soon as the lady who presided at the receipt of custom in the hall learned who her visitor was, she showed a vivacious interest. She rang a bell; a page who had grown out of his uniform emerged from some secret hiding-place, rubbing his eyes.

"Go and call Richards, the night-porter," ordered the lady; "gentleman wants to see him."

Richards, the night-porter, was an obliging, active man of about forty-five. Jago felt that he could not conduct his inquiry with two curious people listening to every word.

He turned to the lady. "I should like to see the night-porter alone, ma'am, if you have a room vacant."

"Certainly; there's no one in the coffee-room at this hour. Richards will take you there."

As soon as every door was shut Jago pulled out his notebook and began his interrogation. "They say that you remember the evening of Saturday, September 29?"

"Yes, I remember it well. You mean the night when a gent came in late with his clothes and boots thick with mud and asked me to clean them. Nice gentleman, he was, and what he wanted messing about in the bogs on the moor I don't know. He told me that he'd been trying for a short cut; that's how they all get bogged up there—trying a short cut, and it's the longest cut in the end."

"Did he say what part of the moor it was where he got bogged?"

"I understood him to say that it was on the south side of North Hessary, and that he plumped right into the bog before he knew what it was. He said he lost his pocket-book when he fell and wasted a lot of time feeling for it in the mud, and then that his matches were wet and his watch had stopped, and Lord bless me! If you'd heard the things that had happened to him you'd have said he was daft to have gone there."

"What sort of things?"

"Oh, how he went deeper and deeper and the more he struggled to get out the deeper he went, and then he had the sense first to sit down in the liquid mud and then to lie full length; that stopped him sinking head under. Lord! But he was in a mess, I can tell you. I made him undress and get into his pyjamas, and then I took all his things down to the furnace house to get them dried. It took me the best part of the night with a stick and a clothes-brush to get his things to look like decent clothes, but in the end I did it and I don't mind telling you that he tipped me handsome."

"Did you notice anything special about him?"

The porter reflected. "Well no, I don't know that I did, except that he was a gentleman all right. You could tell that from the way he talked."

"What age was he, do you think?"

"That's hard to say. I should put him between thirty and forty."

Jago now pressed the porter for a personal description of the man, and found how very little most of us notice about the strangers we meet. This stranger was just a gentleman with nothing particular about him.

"Did you notice anything special about his clothes?"

"I don't know that I did; they were good clothes made of good cloth, with the name of the tailor inside like all good clothes have."

"Do you remember the name of the tailor?"

"No, I took no particular notice of that, but I do remember one thing, the tailor's address in London. Sackville Street it was; I remember it because I was footman to a Mr. Sackville twenty years ago."

"When the gentleman left the hotel, do you know where he went?"

"I don't, but I dare say they'll tell you that at the desk. Stop though, I ought to know, because, of course, the first thing I had to do with the clothes was to empty the pockets. The gentleman had taken out his pocket-book and his watch and keys, and I suppose his money too, but in a little pocket I found a return half of a ticket to Paddington, and I remember taking it to him and saying, 'You ought to be careful of this, sir.'"

"What class was he travelling?"

"Third, like the rest of us."

Jago thanked him and slipped half a crown into his palm. The porter thanked him effusively; half-crowns were not slipped into one's palm in the Globe Hotel every day of the week.

Jago addressed his next inquiry to the lady at the desk.

"I hope that our night-porter gave you the information you wanted," she said brightly.

"Yes, thank you, and now I want to ask you to give me a little more. Will you look up your register for September 29 and read out the names of the people who were staying here."

She read out the list.

"Did any of these leave by an early train on the next day, Sunday?"

"Three of them left us on Sunday—Mr. Ellis, Mr. Biddlecombe and Mr. Wise—but I don't remember what time they left." She corrected herself. "Yes, of course I do. Mr. James Ellis left in the morning to catch the London train, and the other two had lunch here."

"Was Mr. Ellis the man who had had to have his clothes dried by the night-porter?"

"Yes, that was him."

Jago returned to Winterton not ill-pleased with the additional information he had obtained. There was, of course, nothing to show that the man who committed the murder was identical with the man who got bogged on Dartmoor, but there could surely not have been two so foolish as to tempt Providence by making a short cut to Plymouth by the south of North Hessary Tor. Probably Ellis was an assumed name; that would not help, nor perhaps would the address of a Sackville Street tailor; still he thought he would acquire merit in the eyes of his chief for having employed his time usefully.

On his return to Winterton he learned that a telephone call had come through from Chief Inspector Richardson, saying that he would not be back at Winterton next morning because he had been called away to Abbott's Ashford near Bristol.

Chapter Twelve

CHIEF INSPECTOR RICHARDSON arrived at Bristol too late to do anything that night. He put up at the station hotel, and ordered breakfast for as early as it could be served the following morning. While waiting for his meal he scrutinized the time-table of the motor-bus services to the neighbouring villages, and found that by leaving at 10 a.m. he would be in Abbott's Ashton at 12.30. It seemed to him a favourable time for his visit on a Sunday morning. The whole family would be at home. The father, unless he were a sidesman at the church, would be in slippers and unshaved; the mother not yet making preparations for the Sunday dinner.

Abbott's Ashton proved to be a village of little more than a single street. One had only to walk from end to end to find "Chatsworth," the *chef-d'oeuvre* of the local builder, expressed in red brick with a bay window for the family sitting-room, and a miniature brick tower surmounting the staircase. But Richardson was no architectural critic; he supposed that when the Dearborn family made its entry into this ambitious dwelling, with its pitch-pine staircase and tiled front hall, with its sitting-room in which no one ever sat and its dining-room in which the family sat all day, it considered that it had taken a step upwards in the social scale and was inclined to look down its nose at its neighbours. He rang the bell; a scuttering of feet on the staircase and the whispers of a family in consultation were borne faintly to his ears, for on Sunday morning it was rare for neighbours to drop in.

The door was opened by a young man in the early twenties, who recoiled a little on seeing the tall form of Richardson.

"Do Mr. and Mrs. Dearborn live here?" asked the visitor.

"Yes."

"And you are Mr. Dearborn's son?"

"Yes."

"Do you think I could see your father for a minute?"

"I'll ask him if you like. Who shall I say?"

"Just say that Mr. Richardson would like to speak to him for a few minutes."

The young man seemed to remember the laws of hospitality practised by his elders, and asked the visitor to come in and take a seat. He led him into the swept and garnished sitting-room and went to find his mother.

"There's a gent asking to see one of you," he announced in the bedroom upstairs. "I've shown him into the parlour."

"Can't be the gas man," remarked the mother. "He wouldn't come on a Sunday."

"No, he isn't the gas man, he's a gentleman from London, I should say by the look of him."

"Funny thing," she grumbled; "what's a gentleman from London want with us on a Sunday morning?" Then she brightened. "I know what it is; one of those life insurance gentlemen who wanted to be sure to catch us at home. Well, your dad won't be fit to be seen. I'll have to go down myself. If he minds waiting, he shouldn't have come."

The lady prepared herself to be a family sacrifice, as Richardson could tell from the quaking of the ceiling above him and the jingling of the glass chandelier. The builder had saved money on the rafters. Presently the footfalls were transferred to the pitch-pine staircase, which seemed to be the solidest part of the house. The door opened and Mrs. Dearborn stood before him. He rose to greet her. She was a comfortable-looking matron, nearly sixty, grey-haired, well preserved and pleasant-mannered. Richardson knew this type of mother well; he guessed that she would not be communicative with a stranger about her son until her confidence had been won.

"I may be bringing you bad news, madam," he began; "a Mr. Charles Dearborn died two weeks ago in South Devon and I am anxious to trace his relatives."

For a moment a startled look of horror showed on her face and then she asked, "Are you sure that it was two weeks ago?"

"Yes; it was on the 29th of September." Her look of relief did not escape Richardson's keen gaze.

"He couldn't have been a relative of ours."

"It was to make sure of that that I have called."

"How did you find out our address?"

"Your daughter-in-law gave it to me."

Mrs. Dearborn was too well brought up to snort; she made an inarticulate sound which was an equivalent.

"Oh, she told you, did she?"

"Yes; there would be no breach of confidence if I told you that she is trying to prove that the Mr. Dearborn who died a fortnight ago was her husband."

"Ah! She wanted to know that, did she? You'll excuse me, but I don't quite understand how you come into the business, unless, of course, you're her lawyer."

"No, madam, I'm not acting for her, but for the other Mrs. Dearborn, the widow of the man who died. You see, she doesn't like to think that her late husband committed bigamy in marrying her."

"Oh, that daughter-in-law of mine wouldn't mind what unhappiness she brought into the homes of other people."

"Can you tell me where her husband, your son, is now?"

He saw a look of obstinacy hardening her face.

"I'm sorry I can't. We haven't heard from him for six years."

"Did you send anyone—your other son, for instance—down to Devonshire to ask whether the dead Charles Dearborn was a relation?"

"No, I knew we hadn't lost any relation."

"Then you know that your son Charles is alive, "said Richardson, with a smile to turn away the wrath of a woman who has fallen into a trap.

"Now look here, I see what it is. She's sent you down here to find out where Charles is. She's been trying all along to find him, and now that she's made a pot of money on the films she's employing other people."

"I assure you, madam, that I'm not acting for her, but for the legal wife of the man who is dead. As I told you, your daughter-in-law wished to claim him as her husband in order to be free to marry again."

"To be free? She can't want that more than we do. She ruined my son's life. Ever since she won that beauty competition, she spent every penny he made on decking herself out; when he came home tired from his day's work he'd find nothing in the house to eat because she'd gone off with some admirer to dine and go to the pictures. She ruined his temper by nagging at him, and then one day he answered his boss back before everybody in the shop and of course he got the sack; he was a cashier at the time. Then she got an offer from a film company and said she wasn't going to keep him; he'd better clear out. So he left her and never wants to see her again."

"I quite understand that," said Richardson soothingly. "I wish I could persuade you to give me his address for the sake of my client."

The lady demurred. "If I was sure..."

"I assure you that I won't give his address to your daughter-in-law until your son himself desires it."

She laughed shortly. "He won't desire it; never fear. I don't mind telling you that he's coming round here to have dinner with us, and if you were to look in here at about half-past two you could have a talk to him."

"Why, if he's living in this village I could go and see him now."

"He's not. He's working a milk round near Bath, but he generally gets over here on a Sunday."

"His wife told me she'd been down here making inquiries, but she couldn't get any sense out of any of the neighbours."

Mrs. Dearborn laughed. "I'm not surprised to hear that. There was no one in the village that liked her or would do a hand's turn to help her; besides, nobody here knows where he's working."

"How many sons have you, Mrs. Dearborn?"

"Only the two—Charles and Albert, who opened the door to you."

"Someone told me that you had a son with freckles all over his face."

She laughed in reminiscence. "That was Albert. You never saw such freckles as he had up to the age of fourteen, but they're all gone now. You see, as a small boy he was always out-of-doors, but when he went into an office at fifteen they began to disappear. You can still see them in a strong light, but they're not noticeable."

Richardson rose. "I must apologize for having kept you so long, Mrs. Dearborn. Please believe that I'm very much obliged to you for taking me into your confidence."

"Well, I was thinking of that poor woman you are representing. It isn't very nice for anyone to learn that she's committed bigamy."

"You are sure you don't mind introducing me to your son this afternoon?"

"Not at all. We shall expect you at half-past two."

While Richardson was lunching modestly at the local inn, he went over his morning's work in his mind. He had not really expected very much from this visit to Abbott's Ashton, except to verify the fact that Jane Smith's husband was not the subject of his inquiries in South Devon. There were two men of the same name; that happens frequently enough when the name is a common one; but when it is not, the usual explanation is that one of the two who bear it has assumed it for some purpose of his own. Arguing on this line, it was quite possible that the Charles Dearborn of Winterton had in some way heard the name and adopted it. That opened up a future line of inquiry.

Though it had no actual bearing on the murder case, Richardson could not pretend that the adventures of Jane Smith, who by her own efforts had succeeded in attaining wealth and position in six years, failed to interest him. She might not be a pleasant person to live with, but at least she had character, and no doubt her husband was a poor creature—that very afternoon he would know how poor.

Punctually at half-past two he was back at Chatsworth, and the boy who had parted with his freckles showed him into the dining-room. The family party was sitting round the fire; the room was heavy with tobacco smoke. Mrs. Dearborn presented the guest to her husband and son.

"I've explained to my son how I came to give his secret away, and he agrees that for the sake of that poor woman down in Devonshire I could not have done anything else."

Richardson was looking curiously at this Charles Dearborn. He was very much as he had imagined him—a poor, backboneless man of irreproachable honesty, of an affectionate disposition, but entirely devoid of the driving-power required for success in modern life. That was why his progress had always been downhill, until now he rose almost when other people were going to bed, to drive a car round the farms near Bath collecting milk for the city dairies. He looked almost old enough to be the father of his younger brother.

After a little desultory conversation with Mr. Dearborn senior, to whom he had taken a liking, Richardson decided to lay his cards on the table.

"I ought to tell you that I am not a lawyer or any of those professions that you may have thought of. I am a Chief Inspector from Scotland Yard, engaged in solving the mystery of the late Charles Dearborn's death." He felt rather than saw the electric wave of excitement created by his words. "The Charles Dearborn of Winterton met with a violent death, though the coroner's jury ascribed it to a motor accident."

Mrs. Dearborn's expression became portentous. "If that daughter-in-law of mine came over from Hollywood with the idea of being free to marry again, and heard that a man of her husband's name was living down there, what with her head being full of gangsters and hold-up men, she might well have had a hand in it."

"Oh, come, Mother," said her husband; "that's going a little too far."

"If you'd read as many detective stories as I have, Father," said his eldest son, "you wouldn't be surprised at anything."

Richardson smiled. "I don't think we can accuse the lady who now calls herself Jane Smith of anything like that. The dead man came to Winterton about three years ago. Can you think of anyone whom you knew three years ago, who might have borrowed your name, because we don't think he had any right to the name under which he was passing."

"Three years ago? Why, that's about the time that I took on my present job, isn't it, Mother?"

"Yes, but you weren't seeing anyone but the farmers when they took you with them on the milk round."

"I believe that when you were in Bristol you were a cashier in a big shop," said Richardson. "Have you had any job as a cashier since?"

The young man shook his head. "No, you can't get that kind of job without a reference. I went to Bath for a bit to get away from my wife, but I couldn't get work for some time and my mother had to send me money. I was ready to take anything that offered. I watched the advertisement columns every morning, and at last I came down to being a cleaner in the Pump Room."

"I believe I could have got his employer in Bristol to take him back again," broke in the father, "but he wouldn't come back to work here for fear of running across that wife of his."

"You never acted as private chauffeur or servant to anyone? I ask this because the man who was killed at Winterton was a man of means and might have employed you and afterwards used your name."

"No, I had to take all kinds of jobs because beggars can't be choosers, but I never took a job like that. I've worked on my present job for three years, and I'm sure that none of the people I work for could be passing under a false name. They're all well-known farmers who've been for years in the place."

"Well, I'm very much obliged to you all, but I'm afraid the case is likely to remain a mystery." He turned to Charles. "I promise you that I won't give your wife your present address, but I ought to warn you that she'll leave no stone unturned to find you. She wants you either alive or dead. If dead, she will be free to marry again; if alive, to divorce you."

The old father left his chair and became excited. "Why not, my son? Why not let her divorce you, and be free from her for ever?"

"Oh, let me be as I am. It would all be such a bother."

"Not such a bother as you think," replied Richardson. "She has plenty of money and divorces are very easily managed in America. However, you must do as you think best."

"No, my son," said the father. "You must show some grit for once. Come out into the open and let her divorce you."

"Yes," added the mother; "you've been in hiding like a criminal for six years, afraid to come to your own home for fear of her finding you."

"Well, I won't see her alone; she mustn't come down after me."

With the light of battle in her eye the mother said, "Let her come here and I'll see you through the interview. Perhaps the gentleman will be kind enough to tell her that she can come and see you here any Sunday afternoon."

"That's arranged, then," said Richardson. "I'll let her know."

They parted with mutual expressions of goodwill. Richardson returned to the inn to await the char-à-banc back to Bristol, where at the railway hotel he discovered as he had feared, that on Sunday night it would be impossible to find a train for Plymouth. He reflected ruefully that he had solved a mystery for the film star, Jane Smith, but that he had not advanced a step in the direction of clearing up the murder of Charles Dearborn at Winterton. He spent the evening in writing up his notes of what he had done that afternoon, and as he had no right to spend his time in revisiting Jane Smith, he sat down to write her a letter at her flat.

"Dear Miss Smith,

"You will no doubt be interested to learn that I spent this afternoon in company with your husband and his family. Your husband is very well and is in regular work. I cannot truthfully say that he desired to be remembered to you, but if you wish to discuss with him the question of a divorce, he will be glad to see you at his parents' house, Chatsworth, Abbott's Ashton, any Sunday afternoon at 2.30. He will meet you in the presence of his mother.

"Yours faithfully..."

He now put through a trunk call to his sergeant at Winterton police station.

"Is that you, Jago? Richardson speaking. I've had a fairly busy day and have cleared up what might have been a tiresome false clue. I should have been back to-night if the train service had allowed it, but in any case to-morrow morning I'll be with you. How have you been getting on?"

"I've had a slice of luck, Mr. Richardson. I believe that I've obtained a description of the man we're looking for."

"You haven't?"

"You shall judge for yourself when I tell you what has been done. It is too confidential a matter to discuss over the 'phone."

"Well, you'll find an attentive listener when I come to-morrow morning. Good night."

Chapter Thirteen

It was nearly eleven o'clock when the cross-country journey from Bristol to Winterton was accomplished. Sergeant Jago had looked up the trains and met Richardson at the station.

"That telephone message of yours last night, Jago, has whetted my appetite for details; tell me exactly what you've been doing."

"There's not much credit to me, Mr. Richardson. It was my local knowledge of the moor that gave me the idea that a man who escaped in the direction described by that young woman, Susie Duke, must have floundered into a bog lower down the Tor; I've done it myself when I was a boy." He went on to describe the steps that he had induced the Chief Constable to take.

"So your discovery is that a man who got bogged on the evening of the murder was wearing a suit of clothes made by a tailor in Sackville Street, and that he took a train towards London. Quite good as far as it goes. However, he may have been a gentleman's servant to whom his employer made over an old suit."

"The hotel people assured me that he spoke like a gentleman. Of course there is the risk that someone else, quite unconnected with our case, got bogged that Saturday evening."

"We can't afford to neglect any clue, however slight, at this stage of the case. It means that we shall have to make a round of the Sackville Street tailors."

"You haven't told me yet the result of your inquiries, Mr. Richardson. Did you find out who that film star's husband was?"

"Yes, and I had a long talk with him. Take my advice, Sergeant Jago, and never be tempted to stand at the altar with any lady who has ambitions for the films. If you do, you'll live to regret it."

"Was the lady so very dreadful?"

"Not at all, she was very comely on the contrary; but I couldn't meet her wishes by finding her a dead husband, so I found her a live one."

"She won't like that."

"Probably not, but there are more ways than one of getting rid of an inconvenient husband. One can divorce him, especially when, like this one, he wants nothing more than to be divorced."

"Was there any connection at all between that Charles Dearborn and ours?"

"No, but I don't regard my journey to Bristol as entirely a waste of time, because I believe that our Charles Dearborn had an assumed name and that he took it from the film star's husband, of whom he must have heard, perhaps only casually, but the name lived in his memory. Most assumed names suggest themselves in that way. We are not advancing fast with our puzzle, but we are not actually standing still."

"What is the next step to take?" asked Jago.

"First to get from the bank manager in Plymouth the exact date on which the dead man deposited £25,000 in notes, and then to look up the informations of about that date showing thefts of jewels or robberies of artistic masterpieces of that approximate value. Receivers would not pay for such things by cheque."

"Why not include thefts of money in bank-notes?"

"Because the numbers of the notes would have been known and payment stopped. In this case nothing could have been known at the Yard, otherwise there would have been a hue and cry in the informations. I suppose that Superintendent Carstairs is not waiting to see me?"

"I don't think so. I believe he's out in the car somewhere."

"Well then, we'll go into Plymouth at once, get the information we want from the bank, then lunch somewhere and take an afternoon train to town. While you're packing our duds I'll slip round to Mrs. Dearborn to tell her that she remains the lawful widow of her late husband. On your way you might look in at the police station and leave a message for Carstairs that we have to go to London in connection with the case and will be back probably the day after to-morrow."

"Where shall I meet you?"

"At the station. I'll come on there after seeing the widow."

Richardson found Mrs. Dearborn at home. She received his information with perfect equanimity.

"I felt sure that publicity agent would be proved wrong. But now I have something that may interest you. I think I told you that I found two detective novels among my late husband's clothes. Well, I began to read one of them, and towards the end of the story I found two pages, as I thought, uncut. I went for a paper-knife and then saw that the pages had been gummed together at the edges. When I felt the thickness of the double page I realized that an extra paper had been enclosed as if the pages had been an envelope. Shall I go and get the book?"

"Please do," said Richardson.

She was less than thirty seconds away. "Here is the book and these are the gummed pages, 301 to 304

Richardson felt the pages. Certainly there was something between them. "Shall I open them, Mrs. Dearborn?"

"Certainly. I thought it was better you should do it than I."

Richardson pulled out his pen-knife which he kept very sharp. He insinuated the point between the two pages and sawed gently along the gummed edge. Then he inserted a finger and drew into view a banknote—a Bank of England note for £500. He pushed it over to Mrs. Dearborn to see. He himself knit his brow in thought. This hidden note had an important bearing on his case, he felt sure. He asked her to allow him to keep it for a time, and then said:

"I had almost forgotten that I had a cheque of yours in my possession. Now that I have seen the film star's husband in the flesh, a comparison between handwritings has become unnecessary. Something which transpired yesterday will require my presence in London, but I hope to be back the day after tomorrow, when I will see you again. Good-bye."

He found Sergeant Jago at the station with the luggage.

"I've paid the hotel bill," he said, "but I asked them to keep our rooms for us unless they were really wanted. Our train goes in twenty minutes."

They paced up and down the platform. Richardson told his subordinate about finding the bank-note gummed between the pages of a book.

What does that mean, do you think?" said Jago. The explanation that first came to my mind was that this note was not paid in at the bank with the others because Dearborn was afraid that its number might have been passed into the Yard to be included in informations. He liked to be on the safe side, but his love of money prevented him from destroying it. Perhaps he intended it to pay for his defence if he were caught."

"I think the plot's thickening, Mr. Richardson," said Jago. "If Dearborn belonged to a gang of thieves, it may have been one of his accomplices who did him in for not sharing out the spoils fairly."

"Without going so far as that I think this note may very well become the turning-point in our investigation. Here's our train."

There were other people in the long motor-coach of the local train, so their speech had to be restrained. They walked from Millbay station to the bank, where Richardson asked to see the manager in his private room.

"I've been wanting to see you for some days," said Mr. Todd. "I've been wondering how you've been getting on with your inquiry."

"I've come here this morning, Mr. Todd, to let you know more or less exactly how things stand; but first I want from you the exact date when Mr. Dearborn deposited those twenty-five thousand pounds."

"I can give you that off-hand, because as executor to the dead man's will I have prepared a statement." He handed this to Richardson.

"Make a note of that, Sergeant Jago—May 13, three years ago. You asked me what conclusions we have arrived at so far, Mr. Todd. We think it certain that your customer was passing under an assumed name; that the twenty-five thousand pounds which he deposited with you were not honestly come by, and that his murder was due to his transaction with that money. We are now going up to London to get further evidence about these things if we can."

"But if the money I have to deal with as executor was stolen, would it be safe for me to obtain probate?"

"Certainly, at this stage, though I am not lawyer enough to advise you about the future. It must have struck you as odd that a new customer should arrive at the bank with twenty-five thousand pounds and open a deposit account."

"It did, but you must remember that we bankers have a good many eccentric customers, and the only unusual feature of the transaction was the amount of the sum deposited."

"I think you told me that the money was in banknotes of large denomination."

"Yes, but of course I did not keep any record of their numbers as I do when we are specially warned about them."

"Do you remember whether there had been any warning of a large sum of money missing about that time? You had no list of numbers furnished you?"

"No; even if one of the notes had been the subject of a warning we should at once have notified the Bank of England and the police."

"Thank you very much, Mr. Todd; I'm going off to London this afternoon to check some information we have received, but I hope to be back at Winterton two days hence."

When the two police officers reached London that evening it was too late to make any inquiries. It was arranged that Sergeant Jago should call at his chief's lodgings at nine o'clock next morning, and that while Richardson was looking through the informations, Jago should do a round of the Sackville Street tailors. Next morning the two met as arranged.

"I've been thinking over our programme, Jago," said Richardson. "I'm going to spend the morning in going through the file of informations for March, April and May three years ago, to see whether any robbery worth twenty-five thousand pounds was committed during that period. It will take the best part of the morning and give you plenty of time for your inquiries in Sackville Street. Then we'll meet for lunch at Carter's in the Strand and decide upon our next step."

The period which Richardson had chosen for investigation seemed to have been a very barren one as far as big crimes were concerned. There were, it is true, the usual lists of stolen and missing property, but there was no record of any sensational robbery such as might produce so large a sum as £25,000. Richardson pushed back the files with a sigh; again the dice seemed to be loaded against him. He consoled himself with the thought that his assistant might have better luck than he, but it was a vain hope.

Jago had, it is true, the name of Ellis to put before the tailors—the name given at the hotel by the man they were seeking. If he had also had one of the incriminating garments to produce the result would have been different, but tailor after tailor went through his books for a customer named Ellis without success.

"You see, sir," said one of the tailors, "we make perhaps from a hundred to two hundred suits a quarter, and if a customer chooses to give a false name to an hotel-keeper, you can scarcely expect us to identify him."

The argument was unanswerable; Jago repaired to Carter's in the Strand in dejected mood. There he found his chief equally cast down; again they seemed to have come up against a dead wall.

"You didn't have any luck with that five-hundred- pound note that was gummed into the book? Wasn't it among the numbers that had been stopped?"

Richardson shook his head. "The only notes stopped during the period were small ones from five to twenty pounds."

"Well, we are up against it," said Jago. "What can we do next?"

"I've still one string to my bow, but it's a very thin one. I can't help thinking that the murdered man got the name of Charles Dearborn either from that film star's husband or from the film star herself. I'm going on a fishing expedition this afternoon. I only hope I shall find her at home and without that ghastly creature, the publicity agent." He glanced at the clock. "I must be off now if I'm to catch her; you'll have to play about this afternoon. We'll meet here at, say, five o'clock."

Jago looked puzzled. "I don't quite see what you hope to get from her."

"I hope to get her to talk about the people she knew three years ago—if she happened to be in England at that time."

A fast taxi conveyed him to Arcadia Mansions in less than twenty minutes. He rang the bell at the flat; the maid opened the door.

"Can I see Miss Smith for a moment?" The maid looked doubtful. "She's got a rehearsal this afternoon, sir, and she's resting."

"Yes, but I shan't detain her long. Please tell her that Mr. Richardson wants to see her."

The effect of this message was almost instantaneous. The lady appeared, clad in black satin pyjamas. Richardson rose.

"You're a nice one," she burst out; "letting me think you were a lawyer when all the time you were a sleuth from Scotland Yard. But say, boy, you're some sleuth!" she added with unwilling admiration. "Here have I been paying God knows what to private inquiry agents to find that husband of mine down in Abbott's Ashton, and you go down there and the family invite you in and give the whole show away to you in half an hour. Say, now that you've seen him can you wonder at me giving him the chuck?"

"Have you been down there already? The appointment I made for you was for next Sunday."

"Yes, but I couldn't wait. No one in my profession can ever wait. I had your letter at eight o'clock yesterday morning, sent round for the car, drove down in time to catch the family at their lunch, had a straight talk with them and drove back again in time for dinner. Smart work, I tell you."

"Did you fix things up with them?"

"Did I not, and that in spite of the family treating me as if I was something out of the ash-can, but I didn't care about that. It's the divorce I was after; they want it too. They've left it in my hands now, but I'll say for you that you paved the way."

"How are you going to set about getting a divorce? Unless there is proof of misconduct it is not a very easy matter in this country."

"Oh, don't let that worry you. I'm not going to employ a private sleuth to follow my husband about on his milk round; the poor goop hasn't got it in him to misbehave himself, and I'm not going to oblige him. No. I shall go to America for my divorce. There it's merely a matter of dollars in some of the states. I'll fix that up, never fear. But say, I'm darned grateful to you for having made it possible all in a couple of days, and if I can work anything for you, you've only to say the word. If it was America I'd see the head of your show and get you shoved up, but I guess at Scotland Yard things are not worked that way."

"Thank you very much, Miss Smith, but all I am able to accept from you is a ticket to see you on the screen."

"A ticket? You shall have a hundred tickets. You shall look in any time you're passing a picture-house where I'm starred. I wish I could do more to show you how grateful I am."

"Could I ask you a few questions?"

"As many as you like, but I've only half an hour for answering them."

"Were you in England three and a half years ago?"

"Now you're asking me something. Three and a half years ago? Why, yes, you've hit it. I was here from March till June."

"Did you make any inquiries about your husband, Charles Dearborn, in those months?"

"Why, yes, sure. I was running round looking for him all the time. I employed two of these advertising sleuths in London and they couldn't do a thing, though they made me pay a bill for charges that made my blood run cold."

"Can you remember their names?"

"Why, yes. There was a guy called Prosser and another called Jordan."

Richardson knew the two names; neither was likely to be of any use to him. "Did you employ anyone else?"

"Not an inquiry agent, but I did go and consult a lawyer man and the snuffy old thing told me it wasn't a lawyer's job, and shot me off on those inquiry agents."

Richardson may have shown his interest in his face, for she hastened to add, "It's no use your looking at me like that because I can't remember the name of that lawyer. All I know is that he had an office in Bold Street, Bristol."

"And you talked to him about your husband—Charles Dearborn?"

"Why, what else should I talk to him about? When he told me in polite language to go to hell, I talked to him in a way he won't have forgotten, though it was three and a half years ago. By the way, you're interested in freckles, aren't you? Well, the office boy in Bold Street had more freckles on his face than my young brother-in-law, Albert—if he hasn't lost them like Albert has."

Richardson rose. "Thank you very much. Your answers to my questions may turn out to be very useful."

"My, but you're easily satisfied," said Jane Smith.

Chapter Fourteen

WHEN THE TWO police officers met at Carter's for tea, Sergeant Jago could not help noticing a less harassed look on the features of his Chief Inspector.

"I see you got some useful information this afternoon," he observed.

"I got something that may turn out to be useful if the bad luck that keeps following me about in this case doesn't step in to spoil it all. You remember that my idea has always been that the murdered man was a lawyer, and it was obvious that he was in hiding when he took that house in Winterton. How did he come by the name of Charles Dearborn? I'll tell you. This woman who calls herself Jane Smith on the films was very anxious to trace her own husband of the same name, and with that object, she told me this afternoon, she visited a solicitor in Bold Street, Bristol, but as ill-luck would have it, she's forgotten his name, so the law list won't be of any use to us. When she went to this man she would naturally have given her husband's name, and being an uncommon one, it may have stuck in the mind of the solicitor, so that it came to the surface of his memory when he was looking out for an alias. As you must know, one of the things criminals find most difficult is to invent names. There was that case of Podmore down in Southampton. That man gave the police more than a dozen names taken from firms and streets, all false as far as Southampton was concerned, but all existent in the Potteries in Staffordshire where Podmore was brought up."

"Yes, I remember following that case," said Jago.

"It was an education for a detective officer. It proved that even when a criminal has brains, the most difficult thing for him to do is to invent a good working alias."

"I wish that woman had remembered the name of the solicitor she saw."

"Yes, it's so like a woman. The essential thing we want from her she's forgotten, but she remembers that the office boy had freckles. I'm afraid there's nothing for us but to go down to Bristol by an early train to-morrow morning, go to the police and ask them what has become of a solicitor who three and a half years ago had an office in Bold Street."

"But why not go down Bold Street and look for the office of a solicitor and commissioner for oaths?"

"Because if my theory is correct and the solicitor went into hiding in Winterton, the office will no longer exist. By an extraordinary stroke of good fortune we may even get on the track of the freckled office boy, who is now nearly four years older, and may be the youth who came down to Winterton and saw Lieutenant Cosway. His object may have been blackmail, but we needn't worry about that."

Their first visit after arriving in Bristol was to the City Police Office, where Richardson asked for the senior detective officer. The two were conducted to a room marked "Detective Inspector," where they found a man older than Richardson, busy writing at a table.

"I must introduce myself, Inspector," said Richardson. "I am Chief Inspector Richardson from the Yard and this is Detective Sergeant Jago. We are now investigating a murder case in South Devon; the Chief Constable applied for our services."

The Detective Inspector became alert and obliging; he did not receive visits from senior officers of Scotland Yard every day.

"Has your Devon case brought you so far afield as Bristol?"

"Yes, because we cannot afford to neglect any clue, however slight. The case down there is very baffling and mysterious."

"How can we help you?"

"By giving us any information you may have about a solicitor's firm that was practising three and a half years ago in Bold Street. For all I know to the contrary the firm may still be there, but I have reason to believe it was closed three years ago."

"You don't know the name?"

"No, that is our trouble. We found an informant who had called at the office three and a half years ago, but all she can remember was that it was in Bold Street."

A light dawned in the Inspector's eye. "If you're thinking of one that was closed down about three years ago, it must be Sutcliffe's."

"And where is Sutcliffe now?"

"In prison. They gave him four years' penal servitude for misappropriating his clients' money to a very big extent. I can't remember the exact sum he was charged with stealing, but it ran into many thousands. It was a very bad case. I was engaged on it myself."

"Had he a partner?"

"No; he was single-handed. It was an unhappy business, because he was very popular in the town, and no one would have suspected him of dishonesty."

"It is a very trifling point, but as you were engaged on the case, you may remember whether Mr. Sutcliffe had an office boy."

"Yes, he had, and what helps me to remember that boy was that he had more freckles on his face than anyone I've ever seen."

"Is he in or near Bristol now?"

"No, he disappeared after the Sutcliffe case and I don't know where he is. I'll tell you what I can do to help you, but I must get the Chief Constable's consent first," said the Inspector; "I can have the file in the Sutcliffe case hunted up and lend it to you. The Chief Constable might not like it to go out of this office, but we could set apart one of the rooms for you to work in. You'll find in the file the news-cuttings of the trial. I think the Chief Constable is in his office at this moment, so if you'll come with me I'll introduce you."

"Chief Inspector Richardson from the Yard is outside, sir," said the Detective Inspector; "he would like to speak to you for a moment."

"Certainly. Show him in."

Richardson found a bluff, active man of about his own age sitting at an immaculate office table, engaged apparently in rapid calculations scribbled on his blotting-pad.

"Good morning, Chief Inspector. I know several of your colleagues at the Yard, but I haven't yet had the pleasure of meeting you."

Secretly the Chief Constable was surprised at the apparent youth of his visitor, and was wondering how he could have obtained his existing rank at so early an age.

"Sit down and tell me how I can help you."

Richardson took the seat indicated and explained. "I have been sent down to investigate a murder case in South Devon at the request of the Chief Constable of the county, and the inquiries I have made so far have brought me to Bristol, sir."

"Oh? It must be a matter of ancient history, this murder."

"No, sir; it happened just over two weeks ago, but it leads back into ancient history. It concerns a solicitor named Sutcliffe."

The Chief Constable's manner changed. He was now alert and watchful. "So that case has come up again. You know, of course, what became of Sutcliffe?"

"Only that he was tried and sentenced some years ago for misappropriating money."

"I believe that we have the file of the case, because we had the task of making preliminary inquiries for the Director of Public Prosecutions in London. If my people can dig it out I think your best course will be to read it through and then come and see me again. I shall be particularly glad to hear your impressions of the case, because I knew Sutcliffe personally and I may have something to tell you that you will find interesting." He touched a push concealed under the flap of the table and a constable clerk made his appearance. "Richards, you remember that case of the solicitor Sutcliffe who was sentenced at the Assizes? Can you lay your hands on the file?"

"I think so, sir. Let me see, it was about three years ago."

"A little more than that, I think."

"Well, sir, the file has not been taken over to the old file-room yet. I think I can find it quickly."

"Good! As quickly as you can, then."

The Chief Constable turned to Richardson. "I sometimes envy you people at the Yard. You're not tied eternally to an office desk as we are. I suppose your duties take you out of town quite a lot?"

"I've been lucky, sir, in having to go abroad two or three times."

"Were you the man they sent over to Paris on that case of our press attaché?" asked the Chief Constable with sudden interest. "I read that case very carefully, but I confess that I never guessed the real explanation of the murder until the end. I envy you more than ever."

A double rap on the door cut short this conversation. The constable clerk entered carrying a thick pile of papers. "The Sutcliffe case, sir," he said proudly.

The file had been deep in dust, and the well-meant attempt to cleanse it with a duster had served only to rub in the accumulated dirt of forty months.

"I apologize for the state of the file," pleaded the Chief Constable, "but I dare say that you've had to deal with files as filthy at the Yard."

Richardson laughed. 'Yes, sir; I'm thoroughly accustomed to them."

"Then my clerk shall take them to a vacant room where you can have your sergeant to work with you."

For the first time since he undertook the case, Richardson began to feel that he was starting on the right road. He collected Jago and the two were conducted to a little room near that of the Detective Inspector, who told them that they could work without fear of interruption.

"At last I've got something for us to work upon," said Richardson.

Sergeant Jago looked at the date on the file and said, "I don't see how this is going to help us very much. This man must have been in prison for the past three years; he couldn't have been our Charles Dearborn."

"I may be wrong, but I have a feeling that we shall find out the identity of our Charles Dearborn in this file."

"There's a lot to go through here."

"Of course there is; I've always heard Mr. Walker, who dealt with those big fraud cases in the city twenty years ago, say that there is no more complicated detective work than cases of fraud. What I propose to do here is to dictate to you from these papers a *précis* of the evidence and the summing-up by the Judge. That'll give us plenty to go upon when we are back at Winterton."

They worked steadily through the file for the whole of the morning. The case had opened through a complaint received by the Bristol police, on the part of a lady client, that she had been induced by the accused to invest a sum of £2,000 in the Sulanka Gold Mining Company in British North Borneo, which company had no assets; and that the defendant Sutcliffe figured as the solicitor to the company; that the whole company was fraudulent, since a prospectus alleged that its property consisted of a mountain largely composed of metallic gold; and that no work had been carried out on the property in question.

When this complaint had been brought to the notice of Sutcliffe he had offered on behalf of his firm to make good the complainant's loss, but it had been found that the assets of his firm amounted only to less than £200, and therefore nothing could be done in that direction. The police consulted the Director of Public Prosecutions as to whether the investment of a client's funds in a fraudulent company, of which the solicitor was himself solicitor, amounted to a criminal offence.

In the meantime other of Sutcliffe's clients took alarm and began to press for a return of the money which they had given him to invest, and since he could produce no scrip or certificates showing that the money had been invested, it was decided to take criminal process against him. He conducted his own defence, but, since the cheques entrusted to him had been cashed and the money could not be produced, it could not prevail with the jury, nor with the judge, who in his summing-up expressed himself very severely against a solicitor, an officer of the High Court, having permitted his name to appear and having invested money for a client in a fraudulent gold-mining company. The jury had retired for half an hour and had returned a verdict of guilty. Sutcliffe was sentenced to four years' penal servitude.

"What's your impression of the case, Jago?" asked Richardson, when the *précis* was completed.

"It looks pretty black against Sutcliffe, especially as his clerk had warned him about the real character of that gold mine. It was that company promoter who ought to have been prosecuted."

"Yes, but he had left England for an unknown destination and they couldn't get at him."

"It seems to me that a solicitor who only attended his office for twenty minutes a day to sign cheques and letters deserved all he got."

"Yes, you saw that he had banked very large sums in his private account, and a few days later had drawn them out again in cheques made out to 'self.' That was a curious thing to do, wasn't it, especially in the case of a man who had under £200 to his credit in the bank when the case came to trial."

"I can't make head or tail of it," said Jago frankly.

"I am beginning to see daylight," responded Richardson. "You noticed when I was dictating that this company promoter, Frank Willis as he called himself, had qualified as a solicitor before he took to robbing the poor with prospectuses, and according to the evidence of Sutcliffe's clerk there had been a question of him joining Sutcliffe as a partner."

"Yes; then there would have been two wrong 'uns instead of one."

"Perhaps you had better head your notes with a list of the witnesses who were called at the trial—Charles Instone, Sutcliffe's managing clerk, John Reddy, the office boy, Walter Pedder, manager of Sutcliffe's bank, Lady Penmore—she had given Sutcliffe £500 to invest in the bogus company, but afterwards said it had been a personal gift to him.

"There—I think we can hand back the file to the Chief Constable after lunch and hear what he has to tell us about Sutcliffe. Come along. I'm hungry."

They found a restaurant quite near the police station. Jago was in a conversational mood, for as a young man he had made two trips to Bristol, which was now a bustling modern city. But he found that his chief's attention was wandering, and that he was monosyllabic in his replies. He knew him in this mood of deep thought and forbore to disturb him. He did venture on one observation.

"It seemed to me when you were dictating, that the managing clerk Instone was very anxious to do his best for his chief when he was in the box. It's possible that both he and that office boy with freckles may still be working somewhere in the town. Perhaps the Chief Constable may know where."

"It's possible," said Richardson without enthusiasm.

Richardson's first act on returning to police head-quarters was to go upstairs with the Sutcliffe file and knock at the Chief Constable's door. "I've brought this back, sir, after making a *précis* of it. I find it a little difficult to make up my mind as to the character of Sutcliffe."

"If you'd known him as well as I did, you'd have no difficulty at all. He inherited the business from his father, who was one of the most respected men of his generation in Bristol. He doted on his two sons and perhaps gave them the wrong kind of education at a public school. Anyhow, Robert, the elder brother, developed a passion for travelling in foreign parts. He went off to Ceylon and when his father died he used his share of the estate to buy a tea plantation. Now he is a well-known tea merchant in Mincing Lane and quite well off. The younger son, Peter, passed his examinations for the law quite easily, but nature had never intended him for a solicitor. He neglected his practice, though many of his father's clients remained to him. I don't believe that that man spent more than about twenty minutes a day in his office. His routine was to dash in, sign a few papers, and then off to the golf-course. When I had a day off I used to play with him. You couldn't have met a nicer fellow, but for months before the crash came I had been hearing how he was neglecting his business."

"Yes, but what can have become of all that money entrusted to him to invest?"

"Ah! Now you're asking me something which is not very easy to answer. If you had asked Willis, that rascally company promoter, I believe he could have told you. You see, Willis had a very charming sister, and there can be no doubt that poor Sutcliffe was very much in love with her. I didn't wonder at that—she is a most attractive girl—and if those two had married I feel sure she would have kept him straight and made him work. It's curious how often one member of a family turns out to be a wrong 'un; her younger brother, Percy, is as nice a young fellow as you could wish to meet and as straight as a die, but the elder brother is quite the reverse, although probably poor Sutcliffe took him at his own valuation, and being very deeply in love he couldn't imagine that any member of the lady's family could be otherwise than perfect."

"Do you know what has become of the family?"

"No, except that they have left Bristol. I think I heard that they had moved up nearer London, where Percy has a job of some kind. Of course the swindler disappeared; I was told that he was somewhere in the Far East where people don't inquire into each other's pasts."

"And Sutcliffe's clerk?"

"No, I know nothing about him since the trial, poor fellow. At any rate he's not in Bristol, or I should have heard of it."

"And John Reddy, the office boy?"

"I've never heard of him either since the trial. I wish that I could have been of more use to you."

"You have been of the greatest use, Chief Constable. I feel already that things are beginning to fit together and that in a few days I shall be able to return to London with the case cleared up. If I am in any difficulty, I hope you'll let me write to you."

"As often as you like, Chief Inspector."

The two men shook hands.

Chapter Fifteen

THERE WAS much to be done before Richardson could feel free to leave Bristol. Through the good offices of the Detective Inspector, who had a search made of the newspaper files of the time, he obtained the addresses of Charles Instone, Sutcliffe's managing clerk, and of John Reddy, his office boy. He called at Instone's and found that it was a boarding-house which had been in the same hands for more than five years. The landlady remembered Instone very well.

"Yes, sir, and one couldn't have had a nicer or quieter gentleman than he was. He gave no trouble in the house, never grumbled at his food and was always friendly with the other boarders. He was a great church-goer. The vicar of St. John's knew him well and used to come and see him, particularly after the trouble began over his employer. That case made a big sensation in the town, I can tell you, and poor Mr. Instone was so cut up over it that he couldn't sleep nor eat."

"What became of him after the trial?"

"Oh, he told me that he was going up to see Mr. Sutcliffe's brother in London and try to get a job there. He paid up right to the day he left. I tell you I was sorry to lose him, because you know, sir, in these days one doesn't get so many lodgers of the right sort. I'm sure that he was quite broke up when he had to leave."

"Did he leave you any address to forward letters to?"

"Yes, sir, the Post Office, Charing Cross, London, but nothing ever came for him. He did promise to write to me, but he never did. Perhaps, poor gentleman, he never found another job."

"Is the vicar of St. John's still the same clergyman that knew Mr. Instone?"

"Yes, and very nice he is. If you thought of going up there to see him, I'm sure that he'd tell you all he knows about poor Mr. Instone. I expect he still hears from him."

Richardson's next visit was to the vicarage of St. John's Church. He did not send in his card, because to receive a visit from a detective chief inspector was a bad opening for a first interview. He gave the maid-servant his name.

The vicar proved to be an active and alert man of between forty and fifty. Richardson began at once by asking him whether he remembered a former parishioner named Charles Instone.

"Ah! You mean that poor man who was so hard hit by the trial of his employer, Mr. Sutcliffe. The case made a great sensation in the town. He was sent to prison."

"Have you heard from Mr. Instone since he left Bristol?"

"Only once. He went to London to see Mr. Sutcliffe's brother; he couldn't bear to stay on here after the trouble. He wrote to me that he was trying hard to find work, so I'm afraid that Mr. Sutcliffe did not help him. I sent him the address of one of the agencies connected with the Church with a strong recommendation in his favour, but you know how hard it is for men belonging to what they call the black-coated unemployed to find work. I suppose, poor fellow, he had to sink in the social scale, and that is why he did not write to me again. The world is very hard for people in that walk of life."

"Do you happen to know the office boy, John Reddy, of that firm? They have given me his address as 17 Welby Street."

"Oh, that's at the other end of the town; I'm afraid I can't help you there."

Richardson thanked him and took his leave.

A taxi carried him to Welby Street—a street of little four-roomed houses inhabited by working-class people. The woman who came to the door of number 17 was anxious to give him every information.

"Yes, sir, the Reddys used to live in this house before we took it over. There were just the two of them, Mrs. Reddy and her boy—a nice little chap he was, covered with freckles. Mrs. Reddy had a year of her lease still to run, but she gave it over to us by arrangement with the landlord, because her boy's employer had got into trouble and she told me that someone had got him a job in London. He was very lucky; it's not so easy in these days for young boys to find jobs."

"What do you make of it all?" asked Jago when Richardson had recounted his inquiries of the afternoon. "What was the real name of the murdered man, do you think?"

"It may have been Frank Willis, the company promoter," suggested Richardson cautiously. "He may never have left the country at all."

"But would he have been in possession of all that money?"

"Why not—if Sutcliffe paid over to him all that his clients had subscribed? You must remember that in these days of deflated currencies a gold mine cleverly presented is a very tempting bait. Remember too that this man, Frank Willis, was the source of all Peter Sutcliffe's troubles. I wish we had a photograph to show to Mrs. Dearborn at Winterton, but people of that kind don't spend money at photographers' shops."

"Then you think that the murderer must have been the ex-convict, Peter Sutcliffe?"

"That is easy to calculate. Sutcliffe had to serve a sentence of four years. That means that his minimum sentence would have been three years. He would have been put in the Star Class by the Prison Commissioners, and being in good health he would have been sent to Maidstone to serve his sentence. He was the sort of man who would have earned his full remission. You can do the sum for yourself."

"Yes," said Jago; "he would have been out of prison about three weeks when the murder was committed, but there is still a good deal to clear up before you submit your report. How could the prisoner have known where Willis, alias Dearborn, was living? Who could have told him about the man's habit of motoring to Moorstead to pay the men in his quarry?"

"I know. We are not half through the case yet. The first thing to do is to get from Maidstone the actual date on which Sutcliffe was discharged. No doubt a man like that would have been relieved of the condition of a monthly report to the police. He would have been a free man from the date of his discharge. Naturally he would first have applied to his brother for help."

"You mean the brother in Mincing Lane?"

"Exactly. At that hotel where he stayed in Plymouth he registered under the name of Ellis, but he may have used his own name when he ordered that suit of clothes in Sackville Street. While I go to Maidstone to get his date of discharge, you must make a second tour of the tailors in Sackville Street and find out whether any of them made a suit of clothes for a man named Sutcliffe. Then you can find the brother's address in Mincing Lane in the directory and I'll meet you at Carter's at two o'clock to-morrow. Whichever of us gets there first will wait for the other. We must get back to London to-night. Luckily we can both sleep on a train journey."

"Are you going to look in at C.O. before going on to Maidstone?"

"No, I'll wait until we've something more definite to tell them."

Next morning Richardson took an early train to Maidstone and made straight for the prison, where he was told that the Governor was in the adjudication-room, but would soon be at liberty. In the meantime, if he cared to see the chief warder...?

He accepted the gatekeeper's offer and the chief warder was sent for. Richardson explained the object of his visit.

"You've come about Sutcliffe. Has he been getting into trouble again? I should never have thought it," said the chief warder. "He was one of our model prisoners."

"On what day was he discharged?"

"I'll look it up," replied the chief warder, taking down a book from the shelf and murmuring, "Sutcliffe...Sutcliffe...here we are. He went out on September 7; he was the only convict discharged that morning. But here comes the Governor. I'll introduce you."

"Come into my room," said the Governor, when he learned who Richardson was. "I'm always glad to help you people from Scotland Yard when I can."

"Thank you, sir. The chief warder has told me that the convict Peter Sutcliffe was discharged on September 7."

"I hope that you're not on his track for a new offence. I had a long talk with him before he went out and asked him what he intended to do for a living now that his business had come to an end. He was perfectly frank; said that everybody had been very kind to him in the prison and that all he wanted was to make a new life for himself. He said that fortunately he still had loyal friends who believed in him and thought his sentence unjust. So many convicts say that; I was not impressed, but I did say that in his case, he seemed to have had a fair trial. 'Yes,' he admitted, 'the trial was fair, but it never got to the bottom of my case.' 'Do you mean that you were wrongfully convicted?' I asked him. 'In one sense yes, but in another I was guilty. I neglected my business and altogether behaved like a fool. The fact was that I was quite unfit to be a solicitor.' That is word for word what he told me."

"Did he receive any visits while he was here?"

"Yes, he was visited once by his brother, who seems to be well known in the city, and once by a young woman—a lady and a very charming one. She asked to see me before applying to see him; she thought that he might decline to see her under such humiliating conditions as the prison rules lay down. She told me frankly that the prisoner Sutcliffe had come to grief through being too good-natured and too easily persuaded. 'Weakness of character,' I suggested, but she wouldn't have that. She said that in all the essential things he was a man of scrupulous honour. I said, 'You've come all this way; surely it would be a pity if you went back without seeing him.' 'I won't see him if it will give him pain,' she said.

"Well, I sent for Sutcliffe and saw him in the corridor outside. I told him that I was going to stretch a point and would allow the visit to take place not in the ordinary visiting-room with a wire screen between him and his visitor, but in an ordinary room, in sight but not in hearing of the prison officer. I could see that he was deeply moved by the girl having come to see him at all, but he gulped down his emotion and stammered out a few words of thanks."

"Do you remember her name?" asked Richardson.

"No, but I can give it to you. All visitors have to give their names and addresses." He rang the bell and a clerk came in. "Has the penal record of Peter Sutcliffe gone back to the Home Office yet?"

"Yes, sir, it went last week."

"Then bring me the gate-book. I want to give this gentleman the name and address of a visitor to Sutcliffe in June or July last."

"Very good, sir."

"I suppose it would be indiscreet of me to ask you why he has now become the object of inquiry?"

"It is too soon to say whether he was mixed up in a case that I am investigating in South Devon, sir. He may not have been concerned in it at all, but one has to cover every possibility and make a vast number of quite irrelevant inquiries," said Richardson, who had recognized the Governor as being one of those humane and sensible men who can control a prison better than they can their own tongues.

The clerk returned carrying a slip of paper. The Governor read it and passed it to Richardson. "This is the name you wanted, Chief Inspector. 'Miss Eve Willis, 17 Brondesbury Road, Bromley, Kent.'"

"You said that you asked him what he was going to do. Did he tell you?"

"Yes. He said that he hoped to find work in a garage belonging to some friends."

With that Richardson took his leave, feeling well satisfied with his morning's work. Two o'clock that afternoon found him at Carter's, where Sergeant Jago was awaiting him. The sergeant quickly made his analysis of his chief's expression and knew that he had been successful beyond his hopes; but he began by making his report upon his own morning's work.

"I had no difficulty with the tailors in Sackville Street, Chief Inspector. Langridge & West was the name upon that coat. They told me that they had been making clothes for years for Mr. Sutcliffe of Mincing Lane and Park Lane. They looked up their client's account and showed it to me. Apparently that elder brother is a very dressy man; he had had no less than six suits within the last two months. I asked whether he ever brought in a friend to be measured. I was told that Mr. Sutcliffe had recommended several of his friends to patronize the firm, but he had never brought any of them with him to be measured."

"Then I suppose that the suit which had to be cleaned in that Plymouth hotel was an old one which he had given to his brother."

"No doubt it was. I have Sutcliffe's Park Lane address, but I haven't called there because I thought you had better do that yourself. It's one of those brand new flats that they're building at the lower end of Park Lane. I have an idea, sir, that you have something very much more interesting to tell me."

"I've got a good deal of detailed information about Sutcliffe from the Governor of the convict prison, who gave him an excellent character. He was liberated on September 7, which, of course, gave him ample time to run down to Dartmoor on the 29th, the day of the murder. I have also got the address of some friends of his in Bromley, Kent; a lady to whom he is very much attached. If we don't find him with his brother in Park Lane, we will try to get into touch with him through that lady."

"To me the case seems to be as plain as a pikestaff," said Jago. "The man passing under the name of Charles Dearborn must have been that company promoter, Frank Willis, who had every reason for hiding himself under a false name. When he took it he little guessed that it was to be a sentence of death to him."

"And you think that Peter Sutcliffe had discovered this and lay in wait for him on the way back from the quarry near Moorstead. To me it is a little difficult to fit in your theory with the character I got of Sutcliffe from the Governor of the prison. This company promoter, we must remember, is the elder brother of the young woman to whom Sutcliffe is attached; it would be a bad beginning for their married life if he celebrated his liberation by killing this girl's brother. No, I feel it in my bones that somehow we're on the wrong track, and yet if you ask me where we've gone wrong, I should be at a loss to tell you."

"Oh, Lord!" groaned the sergeant. "I did think we had touched bottom at last. It may not have been a premeditated murder; I doubt whether, when he struck that blow with the walking-stick, he dreamed that it would land him in a charge of murder. A good counsel for the defence would have little difficulty in proving to the jury that the blow was struck in self-defence."

"Anyhow, it is safe to say that a man wearing a suit made by those tailors in Sackville Street, who make for Sutcliffe's brother, did have a violent encounter with Charles Dearborn of Winterton and afterwards got bogged in the marshy land at the foot of the Tor. Whoever the murderer was he did stop Dearborn's car in the road from Duketon to Winterton, and for this he must have had a strong motive. If you've finished your beer let us get along to Park Lane and beard the prosperous brother who lives there."

When the lift had carried them up noiselessly to the third floor and they had plied the electric bell of Sutcliffe's apartment, a manservant opened the door.

"I should be very glad," said Richardson, "if Mr. Sutcliffe could receive us on a confidential matter."

"Mr. Sutcliffe is abroad," said the man.

"Indeed. When do you expect him back?"

"Not for some weeks, sir; he is in Ceylon."

"Has his brother gone with him?"

The man stiffened a little. "No, sir. Mr. Sutcliffe is on his honeymoon."

"Is his brother, Mr. Peter Sutcliffe, staying here?"

"No, sir."

"Does he sometimes come to the flat?"

"Never, sir."

"Could you give me his address? I have to see him on some rather pressing business."

"Mr. Peter never comes here, sir, and we don't know his address." He closed the door politely.

"Trust an English manservant to be unhelpful," observed Richardson as they descended in the lift.

Chapter Sixteen

"Well that's that," said Richardson. "Matrimony steps in and defeats all our plans. There's nothing for it but to get down to Bromley as quickly as we can and interview that young woman who visited Sutcliffe when he was a prisoner at Maidstone. Her address was 17 Brondesbury Road, Bromley."

It was nearly five o'clock when they rang the bell at number 17. An elderly woman came to the door and looked at them inquiringly.

"Can we see Miss Eve Willis?" asked Richardson, in his most persuasive tone.

"Oh, she's never at home at this hour, sir," said the woman; "but you'll be sure to find her at the garage."

"At the garage?"

"Yes, sir. Oh, you didn't know that she's acting as cashier for her brother, Mr. Percy, at his garage. It's the second turning on the left and about one hundred yards down. You couldn't miss it."

Richardson thanked her, and as they went he observed to Jago, "Well, we've added something to our knowledge. The prison governor told me that Sutcliffe said he hoped to get employment in a garage. He may be here now. Remember, not a whisper about who we are, or it'll be said that the police are hounding down a man who has served his sentence."

The garage proved larger than he had expected; indeed, it showed signs of having recently been enlarged. Moreover, it was filled with cars, some of them derelict, others under repair, and others again of the latest models. A good-looking young man, who looked energetic, bustled forward in the hope that they were new customers. He looked inquiringly at Richardson.

"We called at number 17 Brondesbury Road just now in the hope of finding Miss Eve Willis at home and were directed to come here."

"Miss Willis is here certainly, but she's very busy. Is it anything I can do?"

"Thank you, I'm afraid that only Miss Willis herself can answer what we want to ask. We shall not keep her for more than a minute."

The young man made no further objection, but conducted them to a little office with a glazed window at which a girl of striking beauty was poring over a ledger. "You will find Miss Willis in there," he said, turning on his heel.

Richardson had settled beforehand how he should conduct the interview. "You might have a look at the cars, Sergeant, while I go in; it'll be less formidable for the young lady if she has only one of us to answer."

He knocked at the office door and removed his hat before going in. She was even more attractive when she looked up than she had seemed when knitting her brow over her ledger. Perhaps, thought Richardson, her capacity lies in other spheres than figures.

"I hope you won't regard it as an impertinence on the part of a stranger, Miss Willis, but I've come to ask you whether you have had news of your elder brother, Mr. Frank Willis, lately?"

Evidently the question startled her, but she did not attempt to fence with it. "We haven't heard of him for three or four years," she said. "Are you a friend of his?"

"No, but I've often heard of him, and a friend of mine was asking about him the other day."

She looked puzzled. "How did you find out my address?"

"Let me see; someone must have mentioned it to me or I shouldn't have been here, but exactly who it was…"

"Oh, well, there's no secret about our address."

"I didn't know whether your elder brother might not have provided the capital for the garage, which seems to be booming."

Richardson felt that he was treading on dangerous ground and that she might well resent the intimacy of his questions, but he had to take the risk. Fortunately any favourable comment on the garage seemed to win the way to her heart.

"I suppose," said Richardson, "that you employ quite a number of hands now."

"Not so many as you might think when looking at the number of cars we have, but my brother, as I always tell him, is equal to four men, and we have been lucky with the others."

At that moment a tousled head made its appearance from beneath a car; the body belonging to it wriggled out and both head and body appeared outside the little office. The door was opened and the man, with a keen look at Richardson, said, "Please book three hours and a quarter against J 2786, Eve."

The girl jotted down the figures on her blotting-pad and said, "This gentleman is asking me when we last heard from Frank."

The man looked grave. "Is he a friend of Frank's?"

"No," she replied; "he tells me that he's the friend of a friend."

"I suppose Miss Willis told you that she hasn't heard from her brother Frank for ages."

"Yes, she told me," said Richardson.

"Well, then?"

"But I've one question still to ask. May I have his last address?"

The man looked to Miss Willis for the answer.

"I'm sorry," she said, "but it's so long ago that I've quite forgotten it. He wrote from Java; I remember that."

"Do you happen to have a photograph of him?"

The girl hesitated a moment before replying.

"No, I'm sorry; we have no family photographs." She was beginning to look troubled; the man came to her aid.

"Miss Willis has told you all she knows about her brother. I knew him very well indeed, so if you have any further questions to ask I suggest that you put them to me." He turned towards the door and held it open for Richardson.

As he was going out, after thanking the girl, Richardson intercepted a protective look on the face of the man, who was dressed like a garage hand but spoke like a gentleman—a look which gave him a clue to the man's identity.

As soon as they were out of earshot of the office, the man turned on Richardson almost menacingly. "Now, sir, have you any other questions to ask?"

"Yes, one question. Are you not Mr. Peter Sutcliffe?"

"I am," he said shortly. He was more on the defensive than ever.

"I thought so. I have been wanting to meet you for some days."

"You're a police officer, I suppose?"

"Yes, I am Chief Inspector Richardson from Scotland Yard, and the man standing over there is Sergeant Jago, my assistant. We're inquiring into the death of a man named Charles Dearborn at Winterton in South Devon. Naturally I did not want to alarm Miss Willis just now by putting any question to her which might suggest to her that the dead man might turn out to be her elder brother."

While saying this Richardson was watching Sutcliffe's face narrowly. Its expression did not change; the man remained on the defensive as before; he seemed to suspect that a trap was being laid for him. "Tell me this," he said. "If you have to inquire into a murder in South Devon, why have you come to us? That's what I don't understand."

"It's a long story, Mr. Sutcliffe. I am one of the numerous people who consider that you were very harshly treated by the Court at your trial, which I have read. You may have been guilty of neglect of your duty to watch the interests of your clients, but that you were guilty of deliberately misappropriating the funds of your clients and converting them to your own use I do not believe."

The man's manner began to soften. "I was a fool to trust people," he said. "For that reason I suppose that I deserved all I got. As you have told me so much you may as well go through with it and tell me the whole story. You say there was a murder; where did it take place?"

"On Dartmoor, a little way out of Duketon on the road to Sandiland."

"Did anyone see it committed?"

"Yes, there were two witnesses."

"And the motive? There is always a motive, I suppose."

"The motive suggested was revenge for an injury."

"And you don't know yet the identity of the murdered man?"

"He passed under the name of 'Charles Dearborn,' but that was not his real name, we feel certain."

"I see. And so in the course of your inquiry your suspicions have attached themselves to me as a person who had an injury to avenge." He laughed bitterly. "So that is the way you reason at Scotland Yard!"

"I will be quite frank, Mr. Sutcliffe. As a man who had an injury to avenge, done to you at Bristol, you were among the 'possibles.' I have come to you in the confident hope that after talking to you I shall be able to strike your name off the list. Where were you on September 29 last?"

"I was here, working in this garage. If you doubt me go back into that office and ask Miss Willis what I was doing on September 29. No, I won't go with you. If I did you might suspect that I had signed to her what to say."

Richardson took him at his word. He tapped at the office door; the girl looked up and signed to him to come in.

"Forgive me for troubling you again, Miss Willis, but Mr. Sutcliffe has suggested that I should ask you where he was on September 29 last. I suppose you keep a diary of how your men are employed?"

"Certainly I do, and very useful it is," she said, taking a foolscap book down from the shelf. "September 29. Here it is. In the morning he was testing the ignition of J 3420, belonging to Mr. Jarrow. In the afternoon he took Mr. Jarrow out in his car to test the ignition and found it satisfactory. I'm glad you reminded me. Mr. Jarrow has not paid the bill I sent him for the repairs. I must jog his memory."

"Would you think it very impertinent of me to ask to see the entry in the diary?"

"Not at all. Read it for yourself," she said with wonder in her eyes.

There could be no doubt about the entry in her neat handwriting; Richardson felt that a heavy weight had been taken from his mind—whoever had waylaid Charles Dearborn it was not Peter Sutcliffe. This charming girl would have been relieved, too, had she but known how much had depended on her answer. At any rate, if "Charles Dearborn" was her brother hiding under an assumed name, he had not been killed by the man she loved.

Richardson thanked her and returned to Sutcliffe, who was standing moodily where he had left him. "I have seen the entries to Miss Willis's diary," he said, "and I am glad to be able to tell you that your time is fully accounted for and therefore you are out of the picture."

"Well, naturally." He was still nursing his grievance. "You said that you were looking for a man who had an injury to avenge. May I ask what injury I am supposed to have suffered at the hands of the murdered man?"

"We thought that the ruin of your business as a solicitor might be rankling in your mind. Now that you are not suspect, I may as well tell you that we had an idea, in no way verified by proof up till now, that the murdered man, Charles Dearborn, might have been Mr. Frank Willis."

Sutcliffe stared at him and emitted a low whistle. "Frank Willis, when last heard of, was reported to be somewhere in the Straits Settlements."

"This Mr. Dearborn only made his appearance in Devonshire three years ago. There would have been time for him to come back."

"If you want me to help you, I shall have to ask you to tell me as much as you can about Charles Dearborn without divulging professional secrets."

"I can't tell you very much because he was an adept at covering his tracks. He arrived in Plymouth a little over three years ago and called upon the manager of the Union Bank with a large sum in cash —Bank of England notes. He gave the manager to understand that these were the proceeds of a sale of house property in London, and that one of the conditions of the sale had been that the purchaser should pay in cash. Then he went off to Winterton at the foot of the Moor and bought a small house. He engaged a housekeeper whom he married about a year ago. She was a lady who had been left very badly off by her father. The only man whom he took into his confidence at all appeared to be the bank manager, who advised him upon his investments."

"You spoke of him having paid into the bank a considerable sum. How much was it approximately?"

"Twenty-five thousand pounds."

"Well, Willis could easily have made that out of me. I could never understand how it was that I had no bank balance when the crash came."

"I think you had better tell me exactly what dealings Frank Willis had in your office."

"There's no secret about that now. We were going into partnership. You know, of course, that he had been admitted as a solicitor, though he had never practised. When I first met him he was mad about a gold mine in Borneo; he was full of that kind of enthusiasm. He firmly believed in this mine himself, but he admitted that big capital would be required. According to his information the heart of a mountain consisted of nearly solid gold, and to get at it thousands of tons of rock would have to be moved. Like a fool I got infected with his enthusiasm. I gave him carte blanche to go ahead with money which some clients had entrusted to me to invest. The end came very suddenly. I had no means of getting any information myself, but I strongly suspect that the whole story of this mountain of gold was fiction. I had strong personal reasons for not wishing to inculpate Frank Willis. Still, I can hardly believe that he would have been such a swine as to rob me of twenty-five thousand pounds and live on it in comfort as this murdered man seems to have done."

"I haven't quite finished my story," said Richardson. "About a year ago the bank manager told him of an investment—a granite quarry on the east side of the moor—which was going cheap. He jumped at it; bought a car and decided to run the quarry himself with a foreman. This meant that he had to visit it at least once a week to pay the wages. He always took the same road from Moorstead to Duketon, and he got into the habit of leaving his car outside the hotel while he was having tea. It was immediately after leaving the hotel that he was waylaid and killed."

"That purchase of a quarry and trying to manage it himself sounds exactly like Frank Willis."

"Where you may be able to help me is in suggesting anyone else who had discovered his identity and might have had a grudge against him."

"Well, of course I was not the only one who lost money in this wildcat gold scheme. I could perhaps give you a list of some of them from memory."

"If only I could get hold of a photograph of Frank Willis, I could get him identified, but I don't want to add to the troubles of Miss Willis by pressing her to look for one. She has already told me that she has none, but family groups are often taken and then forgotten."

"I'll see what I can do about hunting up an old photo. It may take time; I suggest that you look in to-morrow. You may have other inquiries to make in the meantime."

"I have. I want to find out what has become of your late clerk and your office boy. I will tell you why. Your office boy apparently was referred to by people as 'the boy with freckles.'"

Sutcliffe laughed. "I'm not surprised; he had more than his share. But I can't tell you where he is now, nor do I know what became of my clerk Instone. I heard that my brother took them both into his office in Mincing Lane; they may still be there."

"That point can easily be cleared up, Mr. Sutcliffe. I am particularly anxious to see the boy, because it appears that a young man extensively marked by freckles turned up at Winterton a day or two after the murder and asked for Charles Dearborn's address, and on hearing that he was dead, changed colour and walked back to the station without another word. Now, I have kept you from your work long enough. I will call again to-morrow afternoon at about this time."

"I am very much obliged to you, Mr. Richardson, and you may be sure I will do all in my power to help you. Will you do me one favour? Will you deal with these questions through me and not through Miss Willis? You will agree, I think, that she ought to be spared anxiety until we are more sure of our ground."

"Certainly I will promise that. And now I must call that unfortunate sergeant of mine, who has been studying the anatomy of every make of car for a good half-hour. Good-bye."

Chapter Seventeen

Sergeant Jago found his chief strangely reticent on their return journey to Victoria. He himself began to feel, not exactly a lack of confidence in his superior, but uneasiness as to how far he might be allowing his instinct to take the place of ascertained facts that could be proved in a court of justice. Also, he feared lest Richardson's reputation as an investigator of difficult cases might suffer at headquarters. He hazarded a hint of doubt.

"I suppose that you entirely cleared away any suspicion against Peter Sutcliffe as the murderer."

"Entirely."

"But that muddy suit which was bought in Sackville Street?"

"Whoever bought that, it was never worn by Peter Sutcliffe."

"H'm!" grunted Jago doubtfully. "I wish that I could feel as sure as you do. I can't forget that the only thing we've had to go upon is the supposition that the man who called himself Charles Dearborn took that name because he had once heard it when Jane Smith went to Sutcliffe's office to ask him to look for her husband."

Richardson grunted his acquiescence and added that in a case where one had no certain clue to go upon, one had to make deductions and to work upon theories. "Anyhow," he added, "this case is the most interesting that I have yet had to work upon and I am determined to hunt down Frank Willis at all costs, and let the Department go hang."

"What's going to be your next step?" asked Jago.

"We are going to Mincing Lane to see what they can tell us about those two people who lost their jobs when Peter Sutcliffe was convicted—Instone the clerk, and the freckled boy. You know why we want to trace the freckled boy; he was seen at Winterton: and I want to see Instone because he may be able to tell us something about Frank Willis."

In Mincing Lane there came a check. The cashier to whom they were taken explained that his employer was away upon a long honeymoon. He himself had no very clear recollection of what became of Instone. He understood that his work in a solicitor's office was no qualification for a business such as theirs, and that Mr. Sutcliffe had given him recommendations to other firms in the city, but he did not know which of them had accepted his services. As for the boy, John Reddy, he had very quickly mastered his duties, but after working for the firm for twelve months, he had left in order to "better himself." That was all he was able to tell them.

"What about advertising for those two people, Instone and Reddy?" said Jago.

"Yes, we'll go to an advertisement agency at once. After that I want to clear up one point on which only the real Mrs. Dearborn can enlighten me."

"You mean that film star who calls herself Jane Smith?"

"Yes. Only she can tell us whether the Bristol solicitor she called upon was Sutcliffe in Bold Street. You will remember that when I last saw her she couldn't recall the name of the solicitor she saw in Bristol—only the street. I'm going to jog her memory."

After their visit to the advertisement agency, the District Railway carried them to within walking distance of Arcadia Mansions. As they went up in the lift Richardson explained to his companion that he was going to see a type of Americanized Englishwoman quite unfamiliar to him. They rang the bell; Miss Smith's maid came to the door.

"You will remember me," said Richardson. "I'm sure that Miss Smith will see me if she's at liberty."

"I'll have to announce you, sir. Miss Smith has two gentlemen with her at the moment. I'll let her know quietly that you're here."

"Is one of them her publicity agent? Because if so I'd rather call at some other time."

"Oh, no, sir! I fancy they're naval officers."

The two waited in the little hall while the maid went to announce them. She returned beaming, and invited them to go into the sitting-room.

It was an intimate cocktail-party that they had broken in upon. One of the guests greeted Richardson rather sheepishly; it was Lieutenant Cosway.

"It's a regular family party, Miss Smith. We are all sleuthing. You see, sleuths always hunt in couples. Chief Inspector Richardson has...?"

"Sergeant Jago of the C.I.D."

"Exactly; and I have Lieutenant Penmore of the Royal Navy."

"Never mind about sleuthing," said the hostess. "We're here to enjoy ourselves. I don't know what kind of cocktail you prefer, you two gentlemen from the Yard, but if you're wise you'll let me mix one of my own for you."

Richardson tasted the beverage and pronounced it beyond criticism. "I have called on business, Miss Smith. You will remember that when I was last here you told me that the solicitor you called upon in Bold Street, Bristol, in connection with finding your husband, referred you to private inquiry agents, but you could not remember that solicitor's name. Was it Sutcliffe?"

"What a man! And what a memory!" ejaculated the lady. "Sutcliffe it was, sure; not Sutcliffe, Sutcliffe & Sutcliffe like most of these lawyers, but just Sutcliffe. He was a pleasant-spoken guy, but husband-hunting wasn't his pidgin. He threw me out."

Richardson drained his glass and rose. "I'm not going to intrude upon your party any longer, Miss Smith, but this I will say, that your cocktails are the last word in inspiration. Thank you so much for your hospitality."

The two naval officers were also on their feet.

"We must be going, too, Miss Smith."

"Now look what you've done," she said reproachfully to Richardson; "you've broken up one of the swellest cocktail-parties I've ever given. Tell me, you'll come again? I'm generally through with rehearsals at this time of day, and next time I won't let you get away so easily."

"May we walk with you a little way?" asked Cosway as they reached the street. "My friend Penmore and I have been doing a little sleuthing on our own account. I wanted to do a good turn to that poor woman, Mrs. Dearborn, at The Firs, and I thought that our friend Jane Smith, alias Mrs. Charles Dearborn, would know whether her husband had had a lot of cousins of that name, but it was a blank draw. Such cousins as her husband had, she said in no very polite terms, were unmarriageable ladies on account of their physical appearance. She said that they had the words 'old maid' tattooed from birth just under their skin—or words to that effect. Penmore will bear me out when I say that she was just becoming unrestrained and amusing when you broke in upon us. She thinks the world of you, Mr. Richardson. Of course that always has a damping effect. But seriously, our little widow at The Firs seems to think that there must be something in that coincidence of names."

"I think there is," said Richardson, "but it is something less than blood relationship. The man who died at The Firs had heard the name and it stuck in his memory."

Penmore broke in. "When you were talking to Miss Smith just now I heard you mention the name Sutcliffe. Was that Peter Sutcliffe, the solicitor in Bold Street, Bristol, who was put into cold storage for four years by judge and jury?"

"Yes," said Richardson; "that's the man."

"What an extraordinary coincidence. My mother is godmother to the poor devil, and Peter Sutcliffe was her golden-haired boy. She never believed him guilty."

"She had given him a five-hundred-pound note to invest for her in that gold mine of his," said Richardson.

"She tried her best to save him. When they questioned her about that note, she paltered with the sacred truth and said that it had been a free gift to him."

"You may be surprised to hear that I have that five-hundred-pound note in my bag."

"The devil you have!"

Cosway slapped him on the back. "I told you that my friend Richardson was the world's greatest sleuth and you wouldn't believe me."

"Do you know whether your mother kept a record of the number of the note she gave him?"

"If she didn't keep it she can get it from her bankers. Why don't you run down and see her? She lives in Bath. She'd be all over you when she knew that you don't believe in Sutcliffe's guilt."

"Then will you tell her to expect a visit from me morrow—that is if you will be seeing her."

"Oh, yes, I'm going down there to-night, and Cosway is coming with me—and by the way, Cosway, we ought to be pushing off if we're to take that train."

Cosway hailed a passing taxi and the two young men waved a farewell through the window. Left to themselves the two police officers walked towards the Tube station.

"You may have thought all this waste of time, Jago, but my experience is that a detective can never make too many friends. He never knows when one or other of them may not be useful. It's early days to be confident, but I do believe that I'm beginning to see daylight. We shall know more when we get to Bath to-morrow, but we're going first to Bristol to see Sutcliffe's bank manager."

"Why?" asked Jago.

"To find out whether money was drawn out of Sutcliffe's account in notes of high denomination. I'll take you with me so that you may hear the questions and answers. Happily we've got a clear evening for bringing our report up to date."

Jago knew these reports of his chief, how they went meticulously through the facts of each case; he sighed as he thought of the work that lay before him, for his chief had a trick of closing his eyes and dictating as if he were reading from some document concealed in his memory.

The next morning found them in Bristol, at the bank where Sutcliffe had kept his account, before eleven o'clock. They were shown into the branch manager's room, who, when Richardson had explained his business, told him that the inquiry could not be completed while he waited.

"That is unfortunate," said Richardson, "because we have to go to Bath to-day, and we may not be back before your closing time."

"I'll see what can be done," said the manager, "if you'll wait here, but it means digging out ledgers nearly four years old. Still, it can be done."

It was done. In less than twenty minutes the manager returned, wreathed in smiles at the thought of how the efficiency of his management would impress these cold officers from Scotland Yard.

"You wanted to know whether money was drawn from the Sutcliffe account in Bank of England notes of high denominations. I have thought it best to have a transcript made of the withdrawals for the twelve months preceding the closing of the account. Here it is."

"It is very good of you. May I take this away with me?"

"Of course you may. I had it made up for you."

In the train on the journey to Bath Richardson took the paper from his pocket and studied it. Certainly it gave him material for thought. For a whole year money had been drawn out of his account by Sutcliffe almost weekly in Bank of England notes, mostly of the value of £100, though twice the denominations had been £500. What could he have wanted so much cash for?

He was, of course, receiving large sums from clients for investment in the wildcat schemes of his prospective partner, Frank Willis, but why should that person hold to receiving money to be invested in his companies in cash and always in Bank of England notes of high values? The Charles Dearborn who died at Winterton deposited £25,000 at his bank in Plymouth all in notes of these high denominations. This was undoubtedly another link in the chain, but did the chain lead to Frank Willis? Sutcliffe would be able to settle the point if he could produce a photograph of Willis which could be shown to Mrs. Dearborn in Winterton, and he would be able to say how long he had been associated with Willis before the crash.

The train pulled up at Bath and Richardson was recalled to the realities of the moment. "We can't break in on Lady Penmore at lunch-time. We'll have to take a sandwich lunch at the buffet and get to her at two o'clock. She'll have finished lunch by then."

A taxi carried them a little later on to the address of Lady Penmore, who lived in one of the picturesque stone houses of a century and a half ago. It was beautifully furnished with things of the late eighteenth century.

The maid stood aside to allow young Penmore to greet the visitors. "Come upstairs," he said; "my mother is expecting you."

Lady Penmore was not at all like the picture which Richardson had drawn of her in his own mind—an old-fashioned lady in keeping with her surroundings. She was weather-beaten and outspoken, as active in her movements as a girl of eighteen; as emphatic in her prejudices as a party journalist.

"So you're the famous Richardson of the Yard? I should not have guessed it if I'd met you in the street. I suppose that under your calm and modest exterior you have more family secrets and scandals tucked away than are to be found in the card index of a society newspaper. Never mind, you may have all sorts of terrible things out of my past life, but I can see by your unmoved look that you don't believe half of them. Now to business. My boy tells me that you are out to prove the innocence of my godson, Peter Sutcliffe, though what good that can do after the poor devil's done three years I don't quite see. However, you've got the proof now."

"Well…" began Richardson cautiously.

"You have my bank-note for £500, and you found it in the pocket of Frank Willis."

"We have not yet proved the identity of the man who was in possession of the note."

"Good heavens! Are all you Scotland Yard men so slow in the uptake? What more do you want? Of course it was Frank Willis; he'd run off to Winterton with his ill-gotten gains and changed his name. Have you got the note with you?"

"Yes, Lady Penmore. If you will give me the number of your note I'll produce the one we found to compare with it."

"Good Lord! You don't even trust me. Well, have it your own way." She went to a drawer in her secretaire and took out a slip of paper which she read out to Richardson.

He was taking from his pocket-book an envelope containing the bank-note found gummed between the pages of a detective novel. The two numbers were identical.

"Well, all's well that ends well. I've got my note back. I'll take it down to the bank to-morrow; it'll help to pay my income-tax."

"I'm afraid that I can't give it back to you yet, Lady Penmore; we may require it in evidence."

"Surely you're not going to try the man who knocked out such an arch-scoundrel as Frank Willis? Why, he was a public benefactor."

"We haven't found him yet, and perhaps we never shall."

"Not at the rate you seem to be going; but if you're going to prove my godson's innocence and you can't do it without the note, I suppose I must let you keep it. I've washed my hands of the young idiot, who first of all allows himself to be bled to the white by that scoundrel, Willis, and then when they let him out of prison goes down to work with other members of that tainted family in a garage. He wouldn't have been convicted if he'd told all he knew about that family, but a man when he's in love… Well, I won't dwell on it, for fear I may use plain English and shock you."

"Do you remember how you sent the note to Mr. Sutcliffe? Did you hand it to him personally?"

"No; the young fool was never to be found in his office. I stuck it into a sealed envelope with directions about investing it, and left it with the office boy to be given to my godson as soon as he came in."

"And Mr. Frank Willis was not in the office at the time?"

"I didn't stop to ask; it would have been too great a strain on my nervous system to have to be civil to the man. I never could stand him."

With the note still in his pocket Richardson took his leave.

Chapter Eighteen

"AT LAST we seem to have got to something definite," said Jago, as they walked to the station.

"I can see that you're relieved to find that there is a definite link between the murder on Dartmoor and the Sutcliffe case," said Richardson with a twinkle. "I hope to have more before the day is over."

They were fortunate in the hour when they reached the station. The London express—one of the best trains in the day—was due in seven minutes. As usual when a train is likely to be crowded, they seated themselves in opposite corners and treated one another as strangers. The carriage filled up; the train pulled out and Richardson composed himself to sleep.

They crossed from Paddington to Victoria in a taxi, since they were already late for their interview with Sutcliffe at the garage, and the Inner Circle trains took half an hour. It was nearly seven o'clock when they reached Bromley.

"Ah! Here you are at last," exclaimed Sutcliffe, emerging from the gloom. "I volunteered for night duty so as not to miss you."

"I'm sorry we couldn't keep our appointment," said Richardson, "but we had to be down at Bristol and Bath this morning and that is why we are so late."

"I have something for you," said Sutcliffe. "You asked me yesterday whether there was a photograph of Frank Willis. His sister told you that there was not, and that was the truth as far as she was concerned, but the old woman who has worked for the family for years and dotes on them all, told me that she had a photograph, a fairly recent one, in which 'Master Frank,' as she called him, appears with his brother and sister. She was very loath to part with it even for an afternoon, but I assured her that she should have it back at the earliest possible moment. You mustn't let me down about this."

"I won't," said Richardson. "I'll get the photograph copied to-morrow morning and give the original back to you."

Acting on this assurance Sutcliffe went into the office and brought back the photograph neatly done up in tissue paper. Richardson opened the packet and looked at it critically. It was like most other family groups of two young men and a young woman, save that the picture was redeemed from banality by the beauty of the girl. Richardson had never seen the body of the man who had been buried at Winterton, therefore he could draw no conclusions from the portrait of the elder brother, which in features distantly reminded him of the sister.

"Thank you, Mr. Sutcliffe. This shall be shown to the widow of the murdered man, or rather, the copy shall be shown, and you shall have the original back by eleven o'clock to-morrow morning at latest. And now I want to ask you one or two questions. How long had Frank Willis been with you before the crash came?"

"When you say how long had he been with me you mean how long had he had the run of my office? Well, the crash came in May and he first took to coming to the office in the previous December—five months before."

"Before December did he not come to the office at all?"

"No—for the excellent reason that he wasn't in England."

"Now, as regards your banking arrangements, was your personal account kept separate from the accounts of the firm?"

"It ought to have been, of course, but I'm afraid that it wasn't. You see, the firm was myself, and any money that accrued to it accrued to me personally."

"You had a pass-book, I suppose?"

"Oh, yes, but I can't say truthfully that I looked into it much. Occasionally I looked at my balance, but I left all that to the office."

"How long had your office staff been with you?"

"Oh, Instone my chief clerk had been with my father before I succeeded to the business. He must have been with the firm for ten years. The boy Reddy came to the firm on leaving school."

"You conducted your own defence at your trial?"

"I did, but I was greatly helped by my clerk, Instone, who virtually prepared my defence. It was he who furnished me with all the necessary information, and it seemed absurd to spend a lot of money on an advocate. The facts were against me."

"You didn't call Mr. Frank Willis as a witness for your defence?"

"No, he was abroad. If you like to put it crudely, he had run away."

"Have you kept any papers belonging to your former office?"

"All books and papers at the office were taken charge of by my brother, and I believe that they are stored away in an upper room or in the cellar of his office in Mincing Lane."

"I should like very much to run through them," said Richardson; "not to make an audit of your accounts, but to look at any letters that might be useful to my inquiry."

"Very well, I'll take you down to Mincing Lane to-morrow morning. The chief clerk is very obliging and I've no doubt that he can dig out the papers and give us a corner in which to look through them."

At that moment the big bell rang in the garage, signifying that a customer was coming in with his car. Sutcliffe stepped to a switch and every lamp flashed into brilliance. A car came slowly in on its first speed and a rather haughty young man switched off the engine and descended.

"Have her filled up with petrol, oil and water by eight o'clock to-morrow morning and I'll come round for her."

"Very good, sir," said Sutcliffe.

And then a second car hooted at the garage door and crept in like the other. Richardson and his sergeant slipped out; Sutcliffe was likely to be engaged for an hour or two.

"Let's stroll along the main street and choose a photographer for copying this picture. The only men to avoid are the fashionable ones who display portraits of mawkish young females in their windows; the smaller men are the most use for what we want."

They found what they wanted in a small and rather humble shop a little farther down. Richardson drew a bow at a venture by sounding the door-bell. The proprietor, it appeared, lived over his shop and was eager for custom at any hour.

"Forgive me for disturbing you after closing time," said Richardson, "but I have to get a copy made of a group which is urgently wanted. Will you do it for me?"

"Let me have a look at it. Oh, yes, it's all plain sailing. I can do it right away and you won't quarrel with the price."

"Thank you. I'll be round between eight and nine to-morrow morning. You'll take care of the original, won't you?"

"You can trust me for that, sir."

"Now," said Richardson, "I think we've done enough for to-day, and bed's the place for us. We must get back home."

The two police officers found themselves in Bromley again next morning by eight o'clock. Their first call was on the photographer, who delivered to them two excellent copies of the family group and the original folded nattily into its tissue paper. From thence they went on to the garage, where they found Sutcliffe awaiting them in his best clothes.

"I took off my overalls and had a wash-up as I knew you were coming," he said. "I'm ready to start for Mincing Lane whenever you like."

"Here is the original of the photograph you lent me last night," said Richardson. "I've had some excellent copies made."

"Certainly you people don't waste time. Let me just put this in the office with a note and then we'll be off to Mincing Lane."

"Poor devil!" said Jago. "I wouldn't like to exchange jobs with him. He's been up all night taking in cars, and now we're going to drag him off to the City."

"Probably if he knew what we have to do he wouldn't change places with you," observed Richardson. "Every man to his job."

In Mincing Lane they were received by the chief clerk, a man who had been in the service of the tea company for many years. Peter Sutcliffe took him aside and explained the object of their visit. The old man laughed and said to Richardson, "We don't have the honour of a visit from a Chief Inspector of the C.I.D. every day in the year. I'm afraid that we had to put the papers you want down among the rats in the cellar, and I won't answer for the state they are in." He gave an order to the porter and took them into his own sanctum to wait. Presently there was a knock at the door and the porter entered, a little out of breath with the weight of the case he was carrying. It was covered with dust and mildew.

"If you are going to open the case in here, sir," he said, "I should advise you to turn up the rugs and have a brush handy. I'll draw the screws."

The rats had not gnawed their way in, but every other agency that destroys records had been busily at work—dust, damp and mildew. Clearly it was going to be a dirty job. Fortunately the books were all at the bottom of the case, and it was only the papers at the top with which Richardson was concerned. He went down on his knees beside the case and began to pull them out, while Jago stood by with a duster.

"What are you looking for?" asked Sutcliffe. "I may be able to help you."

"I want specimens of the handwriting of Instone, your clerk, and of Reddy your office boy."

"Oh, those are easily found. Here you are! This is Instone's—it's only a list of documents, but that will do as well as anything else. And here, by good luck, is a specimen of Reddy's. Now what else do you want?"

"I should like to have any letter from that woman, Dora Straight, who made a complaint to the Bristol police about your dealings with that mine."

"I doubt whether you'll find that. I can't remember that she ever wrote to me. Hullo! What's this? A letter that has never been opened."

Sutcliffe tore open the envelope and read the letter. He tossed it over to Richardson. It was an abusive letter signed "Dora Straight," the very document they were seeking.

"The lady little thought that all this vitriol was going to stay more than four years unopened," observed Sutcliffe, with a bitter laugh, "and that it is going to be used now by the Criminal Investigation Department."

"I wanted it only for her address," said Richardson, pulling out his pencil. "I want to call upon her. You have no objection to me taking away these letters?"

"Not the least in the world."

After thanking the chief clerk and taking leave of Sutcliffe, the two police officers looked up their time-table and made for Waterloo.

They had the carriage to themselves and were therefore free to discuss the case.

"I didn't quite follow what you wanted those letters for," said Jago.

"You've forgotten that we haven't yet cleared up the identity of the murdered man. Quite a number of people seem to think that it was he who was Frank Willis. I thought so myself until yesterday; but we shall know for certain when we have shown Mrs. Dearborn the photograph I have in my pocket."

"Then who do you think it was?"

"I have my own theory, but I'm not going to tell you what it is until we see Mrs. Dearborn again. Anyway, I'm beginning to see daylight. I hope that Superintendent Carstairs will send the car to meet us. We must catch Mrs. Dearborn before she goes to bed."

Sergeant Jago was the first to catch sight of the police car as they neared Tavistock station. "I can see the car," he shouted. "Now we shan't be long."

They had a warm welcome from the driver. "Mr. Carstairs was wondering only this morning when he would see you back," he said.

"Has anything been happening since we've been away?"

"The newspapers have been full of your movements. They've worked up quite a lot of public feeling about the case—making you a 'man of mystery who always gets home on his cases in the end.' They will be deadly disappointed if you don't get home on this one."

"Have the reporters been worrying Mrs. Dearborn?"

"There are always a couple of them hanging about the gate of The Firs. Yesterday she had to telephone to Mr. Carstairs to come down and speak to them." The constable laughed in reminiscence of the scene. "You should have heard him talking to them as if they belonged to the lower deck. He put them through it properly and they slunk off to get away from his tongue."

"Will Mr. Carstairs be expecting us?"

"Yes, he'll be out on the porch as we drive up."

It was a shrewd prediction. The Superintendent came up to the car to shake hands before they alighted. "We've been wanting you back badly, Mr. Richardson. Step into my office for a moment and tell me how you've been getting on."

"We haven't been wasting our time, Mr. Carstairs," said Richardson as soon as the door was shut. "But I shan't be able to tell you our conclusions until I've seen Mrs. Dearborn at The Firs. I think, if you don't mind, that we'll go along there now and catch her before she goes to bed. Then I shall be able to tell you the real identity of her late husband and a good deal besides. Would you care to come with me?"

Carstairs shook his head. "No, thank you, Mr. Richardson. I'll stick to my resolution to leave the case to you, but I should like to hear what conclusion you have come to when you've seen her."

Mrs. Dearborn had not gone to bed. She might have been expecting them, so quickly did she open the door in response to their ring. She led the way into the sitting-room and begged them to sit down.

"I'll waste no time," said Richardson, taking from his pocket a large envelope containing photographs and letters. "I want you first to look at this photograph." It was that of the group of the Willis family. "Are either of these two men your late husband?"

She looked carefully at them and shook her head. "No," she said emphatically. "But what a lovely girl! The one sitting between them."

Then followed the document in Charles Instone's handwriting. "Do you recognize this handwriting?"

"It is something like my husband's, but his was more careless if you know what I mean. He might have written just like this if he were taking pains."

"Thank you, Mrs. Dearborn. That is all I want to ask you this evening. Go and have a good night's rest and we'll have another talk to-morrow."

"But I should like to know a little more. Who was my husband?"

"I hope to be able to tell you his real name to-morrow. To-night you have nothing to do but go to bed and get a good sleep. Good night!"

On the way back to the police station Sergeant Jago began to pump his chief. "Who was Dearborn then?"

"If you haven't guessed I don't think that I ought to enlighten you. But I will. He was Charles Instone, Peter Sutcliffe's trusted clerk."

"But how did he come by all that money?"

"By consistently robbing his employer to the tune of twenty-five thousand pounds in a single year."

Chapter Nineteen

"ARE YOU going to tell Superintendent Carstairs?" asked Jago as they came in sight of the police station. "I could see that his tongue was hanging out for news."

"Certainly. I shall tell him at once."

As they approached they saw a constable who had been watching the road from the steps enter the building, doubtless to tell Carstairs that they were coming. They found him standing at the door of his office evidently agog for news.

"Step in here, Mr. Richardson. How are things going?"

"We are doing pretty well. I had to see Mrs. Dearborn to get her to identify some photographs and specimens of handwriting, and now we know the real identity of her husband."

"Ah! That's something, anyhow. Who was he?"

"A solicitor's clerk from Bristol named Charles Instone."

"A solicitor's clerk? How does that fit in with his being a quarry-owner and a rich man?"

"He was rich because he had been robbing his employer of twenty-five thousand pounds. I haven't got to the bottom of his other villainies yet, but I am confident now that I shall."

The Superintendent was too much astonished by this information to do more than make clicking noises with his lips. At last he found his tongue.

"It's a wonderful piece of work that you've done, Mr. Richardson. I don't know how you did it and I'm not going to ask you, but it's wonderful work. I suppose you'll be able to prove it?"

"Up to the hilt when the time comes, but now I'm beginning to feel that it's sleep I want, and so I fancy do you, so I'll say good night. By the way, if you can spare your car to-morrow I should like it to take me up to Duketon for an inquiry."

"Why, of course. It shall take you anywhere you like."

For a wonder at that time of year the sun was shining brightly over the moor at eight o'clock when the car started on its long pull up to Duketon. Richardson passed the scene of the tragedy with feelings very different to those which had depressed him at the outset of his inquiry. Then everything pointed to failure; now the weathercock was set fair for the run home.

"I want you to pull up at the Duchy Hotel," he said to the driver.

"You had better come in with me, Jago. I shall want you to make a note of the interview I'm going to have with the innkeeper."

At this early hour the bar and the other rooms on the ground floor looked most uninviting. It was being swept out and the granite floors were being swabbed; the proprietor was in his shirt-sleeves cleaning the bar counter.

"I'm afraid you'll find us in rather a mess," he said. "We don't expect visitors so early as a rule."

"I'm not going to detain you for more than five minutes," said Richardson. "Where can we go for five minutes' quiet talk?"

"Come into the back parlour, sir. We shall be quiet in there." He led the way.

"You remember my last visit, Mr. Tovey, when I told you that we were officers from Scotland Yard?"

"Very well indeed."

"And you remember telling me of a young holiday-maker who stayed a night with you and asked you about Mr. Dearborn? He mistook him for someone else. You couldn't remember the name he gave you..."

"And if you've come to ask me for the name now I should have to tell you the same. All I can say is that I should know it again if I heard it."

"Yes, but please be careful when I suggest a name. Don't try to please me by saying yes unless you're quite sure. A great deal depends upon your, answer, Mr. Tovey."

"You've only to say the name and if I'm not quite sure I'll tell you so."

"Was it Sutcliffe?"

Tovey shook his head.

"Was it Willis?"

"No, it wasn't a common name like that."

"Was it Instone?"

"Yes!" The affirmative came almost in a shout. "Yes! Instone was the name. I could swear to it in any court of law."

Richardson gave the order to the driver to set them down at The Firs in Winterton.

"Shall you be wanting the car any more to-day, sir?" asked the driver.

"I can't tell you yet, until I've had a talk with Superintendent Carstairs."

They found Mrs. Dearborn at home. She came out of her kitchen, wiping her hands.

"I'm sorry to break in upon you at such an early hour," said Richardson.

"On the contrary, I've been expecting your visit for more than an hour. I'll just run into the kitchen for a moment and turn off the gas, and I'll join you in the sitting-room."

A moment later she was with them. "You were going to tell me who my husband really was," she said. 'Of course I have guessed by now that he must have been passing under an assumed name. What was his real name?"

"Charles Instone."

She stared at him. "I suppose that that invalidates our marriage."

"You will have to ask a lawyer about that, Mrs. Dearborn. I can't tell you what effect a marriage ceremony with a person who gave an assumed name will have upon the widow."

"Why was he hiding his identity?" she asked. "Don't be afraid to tell me; I'd rather know the truth."

"Well, he was clerk to a solicitor in Bristol and he had, I am sorry to say, embezzled a good deal of his employer's money."

A horrified look showed in Mrs. Dearborn's eyes. "You mean that the money that I'm living on was stolen?"

"I'm afraid so."

"Well then, of course it must be restored to the person to whom it belongs, and I must find a situation somewhere."

"Don't do anything in a hurry. That's my advice to you. Wait until the whole case has been cleared up."

"But this house? At least I can put it into the hands of house-agents to sell for me. I shouldn't wish to stay on here in any case."

"I know nothing to prevent you from selling the house if you can find a purchaser, and that ought not to be difficult. Where do you think of going to when you leave?"

"To London. I believe that it would be easier to find the kind of work for which I am fitted in London than in a country town. I thought of putting the house into agents' hands to-day and going up to London to-morrow."

"Where shall I be able to find you in London in case there are other questions to ask you?"

"In the same hotel where you called on me last time. I suppose that if I should need your advice I could always communicate with you through Scotland Yard?"

"Yes, your letters would always be forwarded, but I shall be seeing you constantly before the case is finished; and now I must wish you good-bye and good luck."

When Richardson informed Superintendent Carstairs that he was called to Clifton for an inquiry, the Superintendent in the fullness of his heart offered him the use of the car.

"No," said Richardson. "It is very kind of you to suggest it, but to take the car over a hundred miles and let it come back empty would be an abuse of your hospitality. We will do the journey by train."

"But you will be coming back here later on?"

"I don't know yet, Superintendent. I have to make my detailed report to my chiefs at the Yard and see what they decide. In the meantime can one of your clerks work out our journey to Clifton?"

In less than five minutes the time-table was arranged. They were to take the car to North Road and lunch on the train. The train connections appeared to work in together.

Richardson glanced at the clock. "I suppose we ought to be off," he said.

"I've ordered the car, sir," said the policeman clerk. "I fancy that it is at the door now."

Richardson shook hands with the Superintendent and the expressions of goodwill were reciprocated on both sides.

"You'll be back again, Mr. Richardson, very shortly, if only to have an interview with the murderer," said Carstairs, laughing.

The trains suited admirably. The two Metropolitan officers found themselves at Clifton in time to interview the lady who had signed herself Dora Straight between tea-time and dinner. A taxi carried them to her house—an affluent-looking one for a single woman. Richardson gave the maid one of his cards and asked to see her mistress on a rather urgent matter.

"It's one of her bridge-party days, sir," objected the girl.

"Tell her, please, that I'm very sorry to disturb her at such a time, but that if they could play dummy for a few minutes that would suffice."

The maid sped upstairs and delivered the message. She must have left the door open, for sounds of protest and indignation floated down the stairs. They caught the words, "But it's not the ordinary police; it's Scotland Yard." A hushed silence ensued; it was broken by a petulant voice. "Here, Alice, you come and take my hand. I'll be back as soon as I can."

"Will you step this way, gentlemen, please," said the maid. She led them into the dining-room on the ground floor and shut the door after them.

It opened again to admit a tall, masculine-looking lady with bobbed hair stippled with grey, and a red face which at that moment was lowering like a thundercloud. "Sit down," she commanded, "and tell me as shortly as possible what is your business with me."

"I think, madam, that you were the writer of this letter." Richardson produced the letter that they had found unopened in the box of papers from Sutcliffe's office.

She took it, read the contents, and glanced at the date. "But this was written more than three years ago," she said.

"Yes, madam, but it reached the gentleman to whom it is addressed only yesterday. He has been away in the country for the past three years."

"Psha! What's the good of beating about the bush? I know just as well as you do that he has been in a convict prison, and what's more, I flatter myself that I helped to send him there."

"By sending a letter to the Chief Constable of Bristol?"

"Exactly. He and his confederate had cheated me out of two thousand pounds, and naturally as I'd lost my money I decided to get even with them."

"You were warned that the gold mine in Borneo to which Mr. Sutcliffe invited subscriptions was a fraudulent concern?"

"I was."

"Would you mind giving me the name of the person who gave you that warning?"

"I should mind very much. The warning was given to me in confidence."

"By a man who was consistently robbing his employer."

"What do you mean?"

"Oh, didn't you know? Mr. Charles Instone, who gave you that warning and so was instrumental in the prosecution of his employer, made away with a very large sum of money belonging to that employer. I feel sure that a lady with your obvious sense of justice will not hesitate to help me by telling all she knows when once the true facts are brought to her notice."

"And in the meantime I'm to be robbed of two thousand pounds on a bogus prospectus and have no redress."

"The two thousand pounds you subscribed to the gold mine will probably be refunded to you."

"Have you been sent down here to tell me this?"

"No, madam; I've been sent down here to investigate the circumstances of the murder of the late Mr. Instone."

"Instone murdered! When?"

"On the 29th of September last."

"Who did it?"

"That is what I have to find out, and I thought I might count on your help. I gather that the warning you received did come from the late Mr. Instone. Did it come by letter or by word of mouth?"

"By letter, of course. I have it upstairs."

"May I see it?"

"Well, the poor man made it a condition that I should keep his letter confidential. He said that in writing it he was risking his job in my interests."

"Yes, but since he's dead, the condition can scarcely hold good; especially when we have to think of justice to the living."

"I suppose you're right," she said doubtfully." I'll just look through the letter and see whether there's anything in it that it's not fair to divulge. Don't get up; sit where you are till I come down."

The letter took some time to find, or else the bridge-party had waylaid the lady on her way upstairs. In the end, however, she made her appearance with the letter in her hand.

"I'm sorry to have been so long. I had to hunt for it. I don't think there's anything in the letter that I ought not to show you. Here it is."

As Richardson read the missive he reflected that this was one of the most sickening documents that he had ever been called upon to peruse:

"Dear Madam,

"I feel it my duty both to satisfy my own conscientious scruples as well as to save your pocket to convey a warning to you. The North Borneo gold-mining company to which you have been induced to subscribe a large sum is, I regret to say, not only a very risky enterprise but actually a fraudulent one. I have read the prospectus with sickness of heart to think that anyone concerned to uphold the reputation of the firm to which I am attached, should invite his clients to put money into a gold mine which does not in fact exist. Many men in the past have been sent to prison for far less than the false statements with which this prospectus abounds. I can only hope to save my employer's good name by warning his clients not to put any money into it. At the same time, I feel that I have a right to beg them to treat this letter in the strictest confidence, since, if it were brought to the notice of the head of the firm, I should be dismissed from my post for the 'crime' of having tried to save the reputation of the firm.

"I am, dear madam,
                    "Your faithful well-wisher,
                                    "Charles Instone."

"May I keep this letter, madam?" asked Richardson.

"No, but if you like to take a copy of it...it struck me as the letter of a man of very high principles. Don't you think so?"

"Before I express an opinion, let me ask you one or two questions. When you received this letter had you paid over the money for your shares?"

"Yes, of course I had."

"You hadn't only sent in your application for shares in the mine?"

"No, I'd paid the money over. This letter didn't reach me till several days later. I think that it was after the shares had gone to allotment."

"Didn't it strike you that Mr. Instone's warning came a little late? If all he says in this letter about his motives were true, wouldn't he have written to you when your application for shares was received, thus leaving you time to cancel it?"

"That, I confess, had never struck me. Then you think that he had some ulterior motive?"

"I do. A Mr. Frank Willis had lately been frequenting the office."

"Yes, Mr. Instone mentioned him in an interview I had with him. He said that he didn't trust him."

"Perhaps the feeling of distrust was mutual." He turned to Jago. "Have you finished copying that letter?"

"Just finished."

Richardson handed the missive back to the lady with a courtly bow. "I'm very much obliged to you, Miss Straight. I hope that you will be able to pick up your rubber upstairs without any very heavy losses."

"Thank you." For the first time during the interview she permitted herself to laugh almost gaily.

As they left the house to walk to the station, Jago remarked, "I give you top marks for the way in which you conducted that interview, Mr. Richardson. Lord! What fire and slaughter she was breathing when she came into the room."

"Yes, the temperature went up about ten degrees."

"But you soon cooled it down. How did you know that she'd had a letter from that swine Instone?"

"It was one of the guesses that one has to make on this job. I'll let you into a secret. If you feel sure that something must have been done, don't ask the witness whether it was done because he or she will say no; speak of it as something that you both know was done and in nine cases out of ten they won't risk lying about it."

"What I can't understand is why Sutcliffe didn't make a better fight at his trial. The truth would have come out."

"Well, you see, he blamed Frank Willis for the whole affair, and didn't want to give him away because of the sister. Instone was cunning enough to use the fraudulent gold mine to hide his own robberies."

Chapter Twenty

THEY HAD TIME for sandwiches at the station before taking the next train to London.

"We shall get in pretty late, or in the early hours of the morning," said Richardson; "but that will be better than kicking our heels in Clifton when we might doss down in London and start work again to-morrow morning."

"What are we going to do in town?"

"Go out to Bromley and make that alibi for Sutcliffe for the 29th September watertight. At present it rests only on the word of Sutcliffe and his young woman, and whatever we may think about it, it won't be good enough for Mr. Morden. Also I want to redeem my promise to Sutcliffe to let him know who the man who called himself Charles Dearborn really was."

"Won't he fly up in the air!" said Jago.

"No; I think you'll find that he'll be stunned, poor devil. He's a standing example of the misery that a man makes for himself when he adopts the wrong profession. If you'd joined the Church, Jago, do you feel that you would have risen to be Archbishop of Canterbury?"

"I don't," laughed Jago; "but I wouldn't answer for you."

The following morning found them again in the garage at Bromley.

Peter Sutcliffe crawled out from under a car with his face streaked with oil. "Oh, so you're back at last; this has been the longest two days that I ever remember."

"I've news for you," said Richardson; "those letters you lent me and the photograph have been useful. We now know the identity of the man who was killed on Dartmoor. He was your clerk, Charles Instone."

"Good Lord! But I thought you said that he had money."

"So he had, but it was your money—money stolen from your account."

"My God! What a fool I was to trust him. But I can't think how he did it."

"It seems to have been easy enough. You didn't check your pass-book, and I suppose you signed cheques blind without noticing whom they were in favour of."

"I'm afraid sometimes I signed them blank."

"Well, then, can you wonder that a man not naturally honest should have taken advantage of your carelessness about money?"

"But he had been trained under my father. I left all the investment business to him. He knew more about it than I did."

"Naturally, but if it will relieve your mind at all I may tell you that his dishonesty over money seems to have begun only about a year before the crash. In that year he managed to embezzle twenty-five thousand pounds of your and your clients' money."

"I can't think how he expected to get away with it."

"I think he felt that it was time for him to bolt, and that was why he was cunning enough to get a woman investor to lodge a complaint to the police that the gold mine you were interested in was a dud one. He trusted that an investigation would be set on foot and that in the confusion that resulted he would be able to slip quietly away with all the stolen money in Bank of England notes of large denominations. And that was precisely what happened. I have with me a copy of a letter he wrote to one of the investors while he was still in your employ. You have it, Sergeant Jago. Thank you. Now, Mr. Sutcliffe, read that."

"My God! Uriah Heap wasn't in it with this blighter. I deserved all I got for trusting him."

"And now, one thing more. I want you to drive me out to the man whose car you drove home on the 29th of September last."

Sutcliffe laughed bitterly. "I see that you won't trust my alibi on that date without a supporting witness."

"You are quite wrong. Personally I trust your word entirely. But I have to satisfy my superiors."

"Quite right. Let us start at once."

He started up one of the cars belonging to the garage and invited Richardson to the seat beside him, while Jago entered the tonneau. They turned into the main road and drove nearly the length of the town before swinging into a side street and pulling up at a tailor's shop.

"You had better get down and make your own inquiry. I'll stop in the car."

The tailor—a youngish man of about thirty—bustled out to welcome a visitor whom he took to be a new customer.

"No," said Richardson; "I'm not a customer. I've called only to ask you on what date you brought your car home from the garage after it had been repaired. I think that a garage hand took you for a run in it before handing it over."

"That's right, but I shall have to look up the date in my daybook." He reached to a shelf for the book in question. "Here it is. I see that the date was September 29."

"Thank you, sir. May I have one of your business cards giving your name and address?"

"Certainly. I don't ask you the reason for your inquiry. I suppose you are thinking of calling me as a witness in some case or other. I hope you'll remember that my time is valuable."

"I will," said Richardson; "but I don't think we shall have to trouble you. Good morning."

"Well," said Sutcliffe, as Richardson resumed his seat beside him. "I hope that my alibi is now watertight."

"Quite."

"Good; then let me tell you of a curious thing that happened this morning. I have had a letter from Borneo asking me whether I still desire my name to appear as one of the directors of the Sulanka Gold Mining Company, and with it was a private letter from the secretary telling me that since the additional capital subscribed by Mr. Viner, the American capitalist, had been invested and shares had been allotted to him, the company was undergoing re-construction. The letter goes on—let me read it to you." He took a letter from his pocket and read, "'The capital subscribed by Mr. Frank Willis and yourself still ranks for dividend, but the directors feel that the board should be composed principally of directors residing in Borneo. As you know, the value of metallic gold is now very high and the new borings through the rock have established the fact that the ore lies in a seam easy of access, and so far without a limit. It is therefore very valuable property.'"

"Then all your good luck is coming together, sir."

"Well, there is a postscript. 'Our sub-manager has left for England and will see you during his stay there. The Board feels that as one of the pioneers who first brought this property to public notice, you deserve generous treatment.'"

"I suppose you'll go out there, sir?" said Richardson.

"I'm trying to make up my mind about that. I must let you into a family secret. I'm engaged to be married."

"I congratulate you, sir. Miss Willis is a charming girl."

"Oh! So you knew that already. Is there anything that you people at the Yard don't know?"

"How was this letter addressed to you, sir?"

"It was addressed care of Miss Willis in Brondesbury Road, which means that her brother Frank was out there at the time. What I can't understand is why Frank hasn't written."

"You don't think that he's the sub-manager who's on his way over to see you?" asked Richardson.

"In that case he ought to have been here by now. He started before this letter was written. It's very mysterious. The question I want to ask you is what I ought to do about that stolen money, some of which belongs to my former clients and the rest is mine. Didn't you tell me that 'Charles Dearborn,' so-called, left a widow?"

"Yes."

"Well, I don't want that poor woman to suffer."

"I think you would be wise, sir, in doing nothing for the moment. Leave the case in my hands and I'll put it before my chiefs at the Yard and get their advice upon it. At this moment we don't know who the man was who stopped Instone's car and attacked him. Until we do, it is going to be very difficult to clear up the case. The person I've been trying to get hold of is your former office boy—John Reddy. I've advertised for him to come forward without getting any reply. All we know of him is that he came down to Winterton on the day after Instone's death, and that as soon as he heard Instone was dead he went off back to the station. We also know that when hiking over Dartmoor he recognized Instone and told the hotel-keeper who he was, but since that time he has clean disappeared."

"Suppose I were to advertise, saying that his former employer in Bristol would like to see him, and I give the address of the newspaper? Surely that would bring a reply."

"I wish you would try that."

They had reached the garage. Sutcliffe stowed away the car and went off to wash his hands while the two officers waited for him. When he came back Richardson drafted the advertisement and took it away to the post office. It was to have three insertions in all the leading morning and evening papers. Sutcliffe ran after him to ask where a telegram would find him if the young man turned up, and was told that a telegram addressed to Scotland Yard would always be forwarded to him.

Then, after arranging matters with an advertisement contractor, the two officers betook themselves to the Central C.I.D. office, and Richardson asked Superintendent Witchard to arrange an interview for him with Mr. Morden.

"Look here, young man," said the Superintendent, "you've been running up a pretty bill for expenses. You seem to have been joy-riding all over the country. When are you going to finish the case?"

"I'll shut it down whenever you give me the word. One can't get to the bottom of a complicated case like this without testing every bit of evidence, and that means running about to interview possible witnesses. This is a far more complicated case than even that garage murder in Southampton. Why not come in with me to see Mr. Morden and save me telling the story twice over?"

"Very well, I will, but I warn you that you'll have to submit to some questioning."

The Superintendent led the way to Morden's room and took him in.

"Well, Mr. Richardson, we have been expecting to hear from you. How are you getting on?"

"I thought it would be more satisfactory if I came to report progress in person. The main fact that can be proved in evidence is the identity of the murdered man."

"If he was murdered," interjected the Superintendent.

"I have found two eye-witnesses of the murder, sir," said Richardson. "This man who called himself Charles Dearborn was in reality a solicitor's clerk from Bristol named Charles Instone, who stole twenty-five thousand pounds from his employer and his employer's clients, changed his name to Dearborn and ran away to Plymouth three years ago, and banked the money on the pretence that it was the proceeds of a sale of house property in London. He bought the house in which he was living at Winterton and advertised for a housekeeper; he engaged one whom he afterwards married under the name of Dearborn. All this can be proved by witnesses."

"How could he steal that huge sum without the knowledge of his employer?"

"I was coming to that, sir. His employer was quite unfit for his profession as a solicitor, neglected his business and spent a great part of his time playing golf. He had inherited the business from his father, who had had quite a prosperous practice. Many of his father's clients stuck to him and would have continued to do so. The crash came when he induced a number of them to invest their capital in a gold mine in Borneo. His clerk, this man Instone, wrote a disloyal letter to a lady who had invested a large sum in the mine and incited her to complain to the Bristol police that she had been induced to invest in a non-existing mine. Inquiries were instituted; it was found that the solicitor had no assets, Instone having stolen them all, and the solicitor, a man of the name of Peter Sutcliffe, was indicted on a charge of malversation of funds entrusted to him. Even then he behaved like a fool. He elected to conduct his own defence, which he did very badly; he was sentenced to four years' penal servitude and struck off the rolls. All this also can be proved. I have a copy of the letter written by Instone to the lady who brought about the indictment of Sutcliffe and the original can be produced."

"Very good. This Instone seems to have been a clever rascal."

"He was, sir. Though he had £25,000 in his pocket, he went about for a week or so after the trial asking for work as if he was a pauper."

"Well, you seem to have cleared up the identity of the murdered man, but not that of his murderer."

"Not yet, sir, but if I am given time I think I shall be able to do that too."

"Have you covered all the people who might have had a motive for killing the man? That solicitor Sutcliffe, for instance? He must be out of prison by this time."

"He was out of prison on September 29—the day of the murder—but he has a watertight alibi which I have tested."

"Had anyone else a motive for waylaying Instone's car and bashing him on the head?"

"I know of one man, sir, but he seems to be out of the country. The person I am trying to get hold of is Sutcliffe's office boy, John Reddy, who would be a very valuable witness if he could be found. I have advertised for him but without effect. I have to-day got his former employer, to whom he seems to have been attached, to advertise for him—three insertions in all the leading newspapers. That may produce something."

"Have you warned the Special Branch officers at the ports, giving a description of the suspect and of this boy, John Reddy, asking them to detain both the suspect and the boy and send them up here?"

"No, sir; I haven't done that."

"Well then, do it at once."

"I will, sir, as soon as I have got a good description of the suspect from someone who knows him well. I learned only this morning that the man is on his way home from Borneo, and I know where he would go if he lands in England."

"I won't ask you what his name is at this stage as long as I know that you are doing everything in your power to get hold of him. It is always better to leave the officer in charge of a case to work it in his own way, but I trust you not to do anything highhanded which may lead to newspaper criticism of this department. I would rather that you failed than that. What do you think about the case, Mr. Witchard?"

"I suppose that Mr. Richardson had better go on with it now that he has got as far as this, sir."

"So do I. If he does pull it off it will make a stir. I'd like to ask you one more question, Mr. Richardson. In what walk of life is this suspect of yours?"

"He's an official of a prosperous gold-mining company in Borneo, sir."

"Then be careful what you are doing, or we shall have all the financial papers on our track."

Superintendent Witchard was more friendly as they went down the stairs together. "If I had known how far you have got on with the case I shouldn't have pitched into you about your expenses," he said.

"As long as you're satisfied, Superintendent, I'll stand any amount of fault-finding that you like to administer."

"I wonder that you didn't think of communicating with the Port Officers from the Special Branch. Send me the name and description of the man you want and I'll get out a circular, not only to our Port Officers on both sides of the Channel, but to the officers at the landing stations of the air lines as well."

"You shall have it this evening, Mr. Witchard."

Richardson looked into the sergeants' room on the ground floor to collect Jago. He beckoned him out into the passage. "Come along," he said; "we've got to go back to Bromley as quick as we can."

"To Bromley again?"

"Yes, I'll tell you why when we are in the train."

Chapter Twenty-One

Beyond calling Jago shortly that they were going to Bromley to get a personal description of Frank Willis for circulation to the Port Officers Richardson was not communicative. He was considering how he could obtain such information from Sutcliffe without arousing his suspicion that the police were becoming interested in his future brother-in-law. He did not relish the duplicity of his role. Fortunately he had with him the group photograph of the Willis family.

He found Sutcliffe working on the ignition circuit of a car—a comparatively clean job.

"We've put your advertisement in," said Richardson, "and I hope it'll bring some response from the boy, Reddy. I've been thinking over what you told me about the mine yesterday. Have you made up your mind to go out?"

"I haven't got further than talking over the matter with Miss Willis. She is all for seeing new countries and says she doesn't mind roughing it in the least; but I'm afraid of the climate for her, and I'm certainly not going out there alone."

"Of course, in the case of your brother-in-law-to-be he seems none the worse."

"No, but it's different for a man."

"He's a good deal older than his brother and sister?"

"Yes; let me see, he must be thirty-eight."

Richardson pulled out the group photograph from his pocket. "I suppose he's not like this photograph now, after spending all these years in the Far East."

"He was very sunburnt when he came home before my conviction. I shouldn't think that he's altered much—these fair men don't show their age, least of all if they have an easy-going nature like Frank's. I did him a terrible injustice in my mind. I thought that he had robbed me of practically all I possessed and that he was the man who had been killed on Dartmoor. When you were trying to get a description of him to fit that fellow, I quite forgot to tell you that he had a pronounced limp which he got from the kick of a horse."

"Well, I shall be very much interested to hear what you decide about going out. Of course you won't go until all this business has been cleared up and the money embezzled by Instone has been returned to its rightful owners. I shall be at the Yard for the next two or three days. Please telegraph to me if you get any answer from the boy Reddy. Good-bye for the present."

On the way back to London, Richardson pulled out pencil and paper and began to draft a description of the man who was to be stopped at the ports. If his surmise was correct and Frank Willis was the man who had had the fatal encounter with Instone, he might be in England still, and therefore must be stopped at the ports in whichever direction he was going. His draft description ran as follows. "A man of 38, fair hair, good features, very sunburnt, about five foot nine, walks with a marked limp. Name, Frank Willis, but may be travelling under another name. This man should be stopped at the ports either when leaving England or returning, and escorted to the Superintendent, C.I.D. Department, New Scotland Yard." He tossed this over to Jago and asked him to make a fair copy of it, for Jago had acquired the knack of writing legibly in the train.

When the description was completed, Richardson cut the group photograph in such a way that only the elder brother appeared in it. This he attached to the notice with a pin. While he was thus engaged, Jago spoke.

"I've been thinking a lot over this case of ours, Mr. Richardson. You don't think that Mr. Sutcliffe's elder brother, the tea merchant, of Mincing Lane, was the murderer? He had a motive of course, if he knew that Instone had robbed his brother and helped to get him sent to penal servitude."

"That idea did cross my mind and I made some inquiries about him, but he is a man who would naturally go to the authorities instead of taking the law into his own hands. Still it was as well to be sure and I asked his chief clerk at Mincing Lane for the date on which his employer left England on his honeymoon. It was on September 26—three days before the murder."

Arrived at Scotland Yard, Richardson went straight to Superintendent Witchard's room. "Here is the notice for the Port Officers, sir. I thought they would prepare a block from the photograph at the head of the notice."

Witchard read the description with a frown. "It's not as detailed as I should like to have it, but I suppose it was all that you could get."

"Yes, sir; I've never seen the man myself."

"There's the limp, of course, but a man who is conscious of it and thinks that he is being scrutinized can generally disguise his limp for a few paces. He can't disguise his sunburn. Why do you say that he is to be stopped going either way? Do you mean that he may be in England at this moment?"

"Yes, sir, because if he committed the murder he must have been here on September 29. On the other hand, if he is arriving direct from Borneo, as may be the case, I'll have to look elsewhere for a man who had a motive for the murder."

Richardson and Jago spent a busy day at the Central Office working up their notes of the Winterton case for the final report. Richardson was not very hopeful that Peter Sutcliffe's advertisement would bring any response, but at ten o'clock on the following morning the messenger laid a telegram on the Chief Inspector's table. Richardson tore it open and read:

"CHIEF INSPECTOR RICHARDSON, NEW SCOTLAND YARD.

Come immediately.—SUTCLIFFE."

He tossed it over to Jago and said, "Shove all those papers into the drawer, lock it and get your hat. This may turn out to be our great day."

They tore across to Westminster Underground station and were at Victoria in five minutes, taking their tickets to Bromley.

No one came forward to meet them when they entered the garage. One or two of the garage hands looked up from their work and that was all. The murmur of voices could be heard from the far end of the shed where two or three derelict cars formed a screen to what might be going on behind them. It was not until they turned the corner of this screen that they saw Sutcliffe, who was sitting on the footboard of one of the cars conversing with a youth with sandy hair and a face thickly covered with freckles. As Sutcliffe left his seat the youth slunk away from him.

"Don't go away, Reddy. I haven't half done with you yet. I want to introduce you to two friends of mine, Mr. Richardson and Mr. Jago."

The youth made an awkward bow, but Richardson insisted on shaking hands with him.

"This is John Reddy, Mr. Richardson—my former office boy and the best I ever had. I think I must have told you about him."

"Are you the young man who was hiking over Dartmoor in the summer and recognized Mr. Instone in the bar parlour of the Duchy Hotel?" asked Richardson.

"Yes," said Sutcliffe," he's just been telling me about it."

"And afterwards you came to Winterton, and when you were told that Mr. Instone was dead you went away without asking any questions. You see, I know all about it," said Richardson with a smile. "Come, come, there is nothing to be ashamed of."

"I just happened to be in the neighbourhood," said the youth.

"Look here, Reddy; you used not to be like this when I knew you at Bristol. Why not tell these gentlemen the whole story and keep nothing back. You see, it will all come out in the end, and if you have kept things back you will look rather foolish. People will think you have some motive for hiding the truth," said Sutcliffe.

The boy looked as if it would take very little to make him burst into tears. "I don't want to keep anything back," he blurted out.

"Well then, you knew that Instone was robbing me behind my back?"

"I didn't know that for certain, but I didn't trust him, and when I saw him on Dartmoor and the inn-keeper told me his name was Dearborn, I felt sure that something was wrong."

Richardson's first instinct was to change the subject and give the boy time to recover himself. "When you left Bristol you went to work at Mr. Sutcliffe's in Mincing Lane, didn't you?"

"Yes, sir."

"Why did you leave?"

"I didn't much like the work, and of course when a better job was offered me at a shipping agency Mr. Sutcliffe advised me to take it. He was very nice about it."

"You never thought then that the change would bring you into touch again with Mr. Frank Willis, did you?"

The boy gaped at him with round eyes. "I don't know what you mean."

"Oh, yes, you do. Surely you remember that day at the docks when you were watching the passengers from the Dutch liner coming down the gangway. It gave you quite a start to see Mr. Willis among them. He had to pass you on the way to the Customs shed. That was the moment you spoke to him and asked him whether he had forgotten you."

The youth's face had changed to a ghastly pallor.

"Let me see," went on Richardson confidently; "I think I can give you the exact date if you have forgotten it. It was on the 26th or 27th of September."

Speaking in a low voice, John Reddy said, "If you know so much about it as that, I don't see why you want to question me about it."

"Don't you? Why, there are lots of things you can tell me that I don't know—for instance, I don't know where it was that you met Mr. Willis in the evening and told him all about Mr. Instone living at Winterton under a false name and..."

"It was at the Charing Cross Hotel, the same evening, if you want to know."

"I thought it must have been there. And he told you that he had never trusted Instone and that he had more than half a mind to run down to Dartmoor and have it out with him; and you told him that you had heard from the innkeeper at Duketon that Instone was living at Winterton; that he had bought a granite quarry near Moorstead and that he motored out to it two or three times a week and generally stopped for tea at the Duchy Hotel on his way back. He said that it would give the man the shock of his life if he were to wait in the road for him and stop his car and then have it out with him." John Reddy nodded.

"Well, now it's your turn to go on with the story. Didn't Mr. Willis say that he would do this before going home to his friends in Bromley, because he would like to get the thing off his mind before he saw them? Well then, I'm going to take down a statement from you which you will sign. You needn't be afraid; it's not going to land you in any trouble."

"But…"

"Oh, I know what you're going to say. You're going to tell me that it would be a breach of faith with Mr. Willis, who is trusting you, but don't let that affect you at all; it's your duty to tell all you know, and that's a higher duty than any promise you may have made to Mr. Willis. You know his address?"

The boy was silent.

"Come," said Sutcliffe. "You'll be doing more good to Mr. Willis by telling the whole truth than by letting it be dragged out of you like this. Of course you know his address—you're corresponding with him now."

"His address is the Hotel Terminus, St. Lazare, Paris; that's where I write to him."

"I can't understand why he doesn't come over," said Sutcliffe.

"It's on account of what happened on September 29," said Reddy reluctantly.

"Oh, we know what happened," said Richardson; "and we've got the stick that Mr. Willis broke over Instone's head."

Reddy fired up. "I can see," he said, "that you believe it was a murder. It was nothing of the kind. Instone attacked Mr. Willis first and he was unarmed except for that stick. He had to defend himself."

"And then he asked you to run down to Winterton again and find out whether Instone was much hurt," said Richardson, "and you went down and asked a gentleman the way to 'Mr. Dearborn's' house, and he said that you were too late because Dearborn was dead. That was what made you go straight back to

London and send the news to Mr. Willis in Paris, and he's been staying there ever since."

"Yes, I told him he was dead, and then I saw in the papers that they'd sent Scotland Yard officers down, so I wrote and told him that he'd better stay where he was until the thing had blown over."

Richardson turned to Sutcliffe. "Do you think we could have the use of Miss Willis's office for taking a formal statement? It may take an hour."

"I think so, but I'll just make sure."

While Sutcliffe was absent Richardson said, "I want you to tell us everything, Reddy. Don't get into your head that you may be harming Mr. Willis. It will be all the other way."

"But if he's tried for murder?"

"He won't be tried for murder, or if he is he is certain to be acquitted. You can take that from me.

"O.K.!" called Sutcliffe from a distance.

"Now come along, Reddy, and we'll take down your statement."

Richardson had now inspired Reddy with confidence. He gave his statement willingly and consecutively. In an hour it was done and the boy was free to go back to his work. Then Sutcliffe took his place in the little office. He had been bursting to ask Richardson a question.

"Where did you get all that information about Reddy's meeting with Frank Willis?"

"Out of my head and partly from you."

"How do you mean, from me?"

"You told me that the letter containing information about the gold mine had been addressed to the care of Miss Willis, and that the sub-manager was on his way to England. That was as good as telling me that Frank Willis might have already turned up. Directly Reddy told me that he was employed in a shipping office I thought that I could risk saying that the two had met at the docks. Of course I was watching his face all the time to see how my picture was going. At the first hint of dissent I should have shifted my ground, but as you saw, the weather was set fair all the way."

"I see, that's how you people get home. It was a fine effort. Now, what we have to settle is how we can get Frank Willis to come over. He is a cautious bird, except in the matter of wildcat investments."

"There is one thing I set my face against, Mr. Sutcliffe, and that is using force. It would be quite easy for us to move the French police to put him on board a cross-channel boat without any warrant of extradition, but then he would come to us in the wrong frame of mind. What is wanted is to persuade him to come voluntarily in his own interests and to make a frank statement of everything that has occurred."

"I see that as far as you are concerned, Mr. Richardson, but I suppose the case doesn't rest exclusively with you. The prosecution would come from a higher authority."

"Yes, if it comes at all, but that higher authority could work only upon my reports and the statements of the various witnesses."

"You think that they will decide not to take the case to court?"

"I do."

"Then it seems to me that the best thing will be for me to go over to Paris and bring him back with me."

"Very well, Mr. Sutcliffe, but you must be very careful to warn me by telegram about the boat you are both coming by; otherwise there may be trouble with our Port Officers. I will myself meet the boat and accompany you up to London."

Chapter Twenty-Two

"Have we got to hang about until Sutcliffe comes back?" asked Jago, on the journey back to town.

"While Sutcliffe is in Paris trying to persuade his prospective brother-in-law to come home and face the music, we'll slip down to Devonshire and take more detailed statements from Pengelly and Susie Duke about what they actually saw when the fight began. Then we have to take leave of our friend, Superintendent Carstairs, and see how he takes our latest discovery."

Having dispatched a telegram asking for the car to meet them at Tavistock, they took the train. They had the carriage to themselves and the car met them on arrival.

"Has anything been happening while we've been away?" asked Richardson.

"Nothing, sir; everything's been very quiet."

"Any reporters up here?"

"No, sir, even the papers have been leaving us alone. When you went back to London they thought you'd dropped the case."

"And what about The Firs? Is it up for sale yet?"

"Yes, there's a notice-board up, and quite a lot of people have been over the house, most of them because they think that a murder was done in it."

At the police station they found Superintendent Carstairs not very much concerned about the outcome of the inquiry.

"Well, Mr. Carstairs," said Richardson when they were alone, "it's been a tough job, but at last I believe that we've got to the bottom of the mystery."

"You have?"

"Yes."

"And who do you think did the murder?"

"A man I have never told you about before—a man named Willis. He's been lying low in Paris all this time, waiting until the hue and cry died down. We've taken steps to have him brought over."

"What was his motive?"

"He had been a solicitor and was going into partnership with Instone's employer. He made up his mind to stop Instone's car on its way from Duketon and have it out with him for embezzling the funds of the firm. He went a silly way to work. He hid himself in the heather until the car came in sight and then planted himself in the middle of the road to stop it. Whether Instone—or Dearborn as he called himself—recognized him or thought that he was a bandit, there is no means of knowing, but I think that he recognized him all right. He jumped out of the car with the starting-handle in his hand and went for Willis, who had nothing but a walking-stick to defend himself with. There was a set-to in the road and as we know, Willis broke his stick over Instone's head, and then made off down the back of South Hessary Tor and got bogged at the bottom."

"Can you prove this?"

"Yes, I have witnesses covering every bit of the way, and the man will be brought back from Paris to-morrow or next day and I shall have his own statement as well."

"So this is the last time I shall see you?"

"Not quite. In order to clinch matters I want to take a second statement from Pengelly and that young woman, Susan Duke, independently. They were eye-witnesses of the fight, you remember. Will you lend me your car once more to do this?"

"Of course. Do you think there'll be a prosecution?"

"No; I think the Director of Public Prosecutions will turn the case down. Still, it was as well to get it cleared up. Your Chief Constable will, of course, receive a copy of my report, and you will see it."

They drove first to Rowe's Quarry and inquired whether Pengelly was still working there.

"Yes," said the foreman; "we have him here as a blacksmith's striker. Do you want to see him?"

"We do, but we won't keep him long. He will only have a few questions to answer and to sign his name."

Pengelly was called from the forge to the office. He greeted Richardson with an air of armed neutrality.

"Look here, Pengelly, I want you to cast your mind back to what you saw on the road from Duketon to Sandilands when the man they called Charles Dearborn was knocked out."

"I've told you that already."

"I know you did, but a good deal depends now upon the question who started the fight. Try to live the scene over again, if you know what I mean."

"Well, as I told you before, we were two hundred yards away, but I don't think I missed much, because you see I was waiting for Mr. Dearborn too. That other man—a gentleman he looked by his clothes—held out his arms like a railway signal; the car pulled up and the next thing I saw was Mr. Dearborn flourishing the starting-handle and making straight for the other man as if he meant to hit him. I think that he did hit him once, but I couldn't swear to it. Then the other man gave him one over the head with his walking-stick and Dearborn dropped like a stone."

Sergeant Jago had been rapidly reducing the statement into writing. He read it over and Richardson handed his pen to Pengelly and asked him to sign it.

Pengelly shook his head. "How do I know what use would be made of it if I put my name to it? I've a good job now and I don't want to lose it."

"You won't lose it," Richardson assured him. "All we want is to get at the truth. I haven't let you down yet and I'm not going to begin now. You are much more likely to keep your job by telling the truth, whereas if you decline to sign your statement it might go against you with the company."

"Very well, then; I'll sign."

"Now to Moorstead," said Richardson to the driver. "We have to take a statement from that girl in Sun Lane."

"Then I'll drop you at the top of the lane as I did last time?"

"Yes."

The girl was at home; she showed no sign of embarrassment when Richardson got her to sit down and began to read her signed statement to her.

"You have nothing to add to this statement?" he asked when he had read it to the end.

"Nothing at all."

"You said in your statement: 'Mr. Dearborn jumped out of his car with the starting-handle in his hand and there was a bit of a set-to between them.' If you were near enough to see the starting-handle you were near enough to see who struck the first blow."

"Why, of course I did. Mr. Dearborn went for the man with the starting-handle and struck a blow at his head, and the man warded it off with his stick and then hit back. But it all happened so quick that I couldn't see how many blows were struck."

"Do you mind signing that in addition to your statement?"

"Certainly I'll sign it; it's nothing but the truth."

Jago had added the words to the earlier statement and had dated them. He pointed to the place for the signature. The girl wrote her name.

"We have nothing left to do now but say good-bye to Superintendent Carstairs and get back to the Yard as quickly as we can," said Richardson, as the car gathered speed on its return journey. "I hope to find a telegram from Paris when we get back."

They found Superintendent Carstairs in his office. "Well," he asked, "did you get all you wanted?"

"Yes, Mr. Carstairs; and now all I have to do is to say good-bye to you and to thank you for all that you have done for us. I shall call particular attention to this in my report."

They shook hands.

"How are you going?" asked Carstairs.

"We thought of going by train to North Road."

"Nothing of the kind. You'll take the car, either to Tavistock or to North Road station, whichever you like. You can catch the express at Tavistock if you start right away."

They did their sleeping in the train and went home to wash and have breakfast.

When they reached the Yard they found a telegram from Paris awaiting them. "We arrive Victoria 3.21 to-morrow."

"Quick work," said Richardson. "It means that I must get down to Dover by midday." He glanced at the timetable. "I can just do it if I start at once. I must be there to meet them, otherwise they will be held up by the Port Officer of the Special Branch. You, meanwhile, can get on with the report."

At Dover Richardson had no difficulty after he had made it clear to the Special Branch sergeant that he would take charge of the prisoner as soon as he landed.

"You'll explain matters to the Superintendent, Mr. Richardson? You see, I shall be departing from the terms of this circular."

"Yes, that'll be all right. I shall have the circular cancelled, of course."

"Do you know the man by sight?" asked the sergeant.

"No, but I know the man who is accompanying him."

"Very well, then, step this way, and we'll get first to the gangway. I see that the boat is signalled; she's on time."

The deck was crowded as the vessel pulled into the quay. It was impossible to distinguish faces in such a crowd, but as the passengers struggled towards the gangway with their hand luggage it became easy to recognize individuals. It was on the gangway that Richardson first saw the man he had been hunting all these weary days. Preceded by Sutcliffe, a tallish, slender man, burnt by the sun to a deep brown which contrasted oddly with his fair hair, was shouldering his way with two suit-cases to the quay. In his well-cut features he reminded Richardson of the brother and sister at Bromley. The Special Branch officer stepped forward to receive him, for he had already recognized him from the description. Sutcliffe waved a hand to Richardson; in a moment the four men were together. Sutcliffe effected the introduction.

"This is Mr. Frank Willis, secretary to that company I told you of; and this gentleman," he said, turning to Willis, "is the Chief Inspector from the Yard who is interested in you."

"I see. His interest in me consists in arresting me, not as they do it on the American films with a six-shooter pointed at my stomach, but in the gentlemanly English fashion which is not even marred by the click of the handcuffs."

Richardson laughed pleasantly. "You are not even under arrest, sir. You are only coming to Scotland Yard with me to make a statement. As to what will happen after you have made it, that will depend principally on you."

"Do you run to a restaurant at the Yard, by any chance? That crossing has made me devilish hungry."

"There is a staff restaurant," said Richardson, "but for anyone accustomed to French cooking these last few days, I can't recommend it. We could lunch on the train."

"No," said Sutcliffe; "I hate a restaurant car. We want to be quiet."

"Well," said Richardson, "we will lunch together wherever you like as soon as we reach town."

"Then I hope that you will be my guest," said Willis. "No, you mustn't decline; it's well understood that at the end of the meal you slip the handcuffs on me, if you want, without any feeling about the claims of hospitality or nonsense of that kind. Where shall we go? There used to be a decent little restaurant near the Army and Navy Stores; what about trying that?"

"Wherever you like, sir; I'm in your hands."

"Indeed? I thought it was the other way. Never mind; we won't quarrel over terms. Come along, Sutcliffe."

It may have been owing to the noise in the train that Willis was silent on the journey up. He had bought an English newspaper and was reading it meticulously, particularly its financial columns. It was not until the express began to run through the suburbs that he laid his paper down to gaze out of the window. At Victoria he took the head of the party and they walked side by side along Victoria Street in so far as the number of foot-passengers allowed them. During that luncheon the conversation was limited to the history and the prospects of the Sulanka Gold Mining Company in Borneo.

"We've more than turned the corner now," said Willis. "I'm not going to bore you with figures in this potty little restaurant where waiters keep their ears flapping when business is talked, and besides, it wouldn't in the least interest you, Mr. Richardson, but I want to tell you that I wasn't such a worm as you thought I was when I mouched off and left Mr. Sutcliffe to face the music alone."

"His fault, as it always has been, was recklessness," said Sutcliffe. "He had absolute confidence that the mine would turn out to be a winner, but he needed money in order to cover the expenses of exploiting it. Even then all would probably have gone well if there hadn't been dirty work with some of the shareholders."

"If it had been six months later," said Willis, "it would have been all right. The money would have been used for development and there would have been something to show. As it was, they thought that they were putting their money into a going concern, when actually no works had been started. I've always felt convinced that the dirty dog in the case was Instone; that he put up that woman, Straight, to make a complaint to the police and started all the trouble."

Richardson smiled inwardly at the thought of the documents he possessed and how they proved the justice of Willis's conjectures.

"He didn't leave me in the lurch as everyone thought at the time," said Sutcliffe.

"No, I left you because I believed that I could do you more good from Borneo than if I'd stayed with you as another of His Majesty's guests. I always believed in that mine and I thought if I could prove it was a sound investment I could get a pardon for you, but I hadn't reckoned on the grind it was going to be without any capital for development. It was an awful feeling out there to know one was standing on a hill of pure gold without the means of getting at it. I had almost reached the point of trying to bore a tunnel into the hill with my own hands—an impossible task, by the way—when I ran across an American, a Mr. Viner, and took him to see the property. He knew quite a lot about mining; he'd been employed prospecting in New Mexico. The first thing he did was to start washing in the creek below and then digging sand out of the banks. There were quite a lot of tiny water-worn nuggets in every pan. Then he went back to the hill and came across what I had always missed—an ancient tunnel in the rock; being overgrown with brambles and weeds I had missed it. The prospectors of those days must have got fed up because the tunnel came to an end forty feet too soon."

Richardson was getting keenly interested. "What made you think that there was gold in that hill in the first instance?"

"The Rajah's wife told me that that was where her gold ornaments came from. Apparently when the prospectors were driving the tunnel they came across a very narrow seam of gold which soon worked out. She said that the tradition was always the same; that the middle of the hill consisted of pure gold."

"I know nothing about gold mining," said Richardson, "but I've heard of people finding gold in paying quantities single-handed—going into a cave and seeing gold stalactites hanging from the roof."

"Yes, you must have been reading magazine stories. It's possible, of course, for a man single-handed to find nuggets in sandy soil. It was that kind of find that started all the gold rushes, beginning with California, but this hill of ours was protected by many feet of hard rock which had to be blasted away before we could get at the gold."

"And so this American financed you?"

"He did. We didn't reconstruct the company to start with, but he became the principal shareholder. Now, of course, the yield has been so big that we can give the original shareholders, of whom Sutcliffe is the biggest, the choice of shares or repayment of their investment. That's why I have come over."

The luncheon had come to an end, the bill had been paid; there remained only the visit to Scotland Yard, where the industrious Jago would be found ready to make notes of a fateful conversation.

"You won't want me any more?" said Sutcliffe.

"No, Mr. Sutcliffe; I think it would be better if you were not present."

For a man who was expected within a few minutes to confess to a cold-blooded murder, Frank Willis was remarkably debonair.

"The truth and nothing but the truth is, I suppose, what you want from me, and that's what I'm going to give you," said Willis. "In that office of Sutcliffe there was an office boy of the name of Reddy, but he was commonly known as Freckles with us. This boy had chanced to see in a Dartmoor inn a man whom he recognized as Instone. He had never liked Instone and when he heard from the landlord that he was passing under the name of Dearborn he liked him still less, especially when he was told that the man had bought a quarry and a car—luxuries which had never been his when he ran Sutcliffe's office.

"You must know that I hadn't communicated with my people for three years as I didn't want them to know my address in case the police came and bothered them. I was landing in the London dock when quite by chance I saw Freckles. He spoke to me and said that he had something very important that he must tell somebody, and that I would do as well as anyone else, so I took him off to my hotel and there heard from him about Instone being on the moor. I tell you it was a shock, for it explained how it was that there were no assets left in the bank. This rascal Instone had stolen the lot. Well, I made up my mind that I'd have it out with him and that I'd prosecute him if I could. Most of all I wanted to see the dirty rascal's face when he recognized me. I thought that I had laid my plans well. I walked all the way from Winterton to within a mile of Duketon, and there I sat down in the heather to wait for his car. It was getting towards evening when it came over the hill. He was alone in it. I ran up into the middle of the road signalling for him to stop. He pulled up, but as soon as he caught sight of me, the little rat nipped out of the car with the starting-handle and attacked me with it. There was no chance of getting in a word. He aimed a blow at my head and I got it on the arm, because I'd put it up to defend my head. Then the blighter came at me again. I caught him one on the jaw with my left hand but that wasn't enough. He was armed with a starting-handle but I had nothing but my walking-stick. I whacked him with that and the stick broke in my hand. He went down in the road like a sack of coal. I hoped that I hadn't killed him, but I didn't want my home-coming to be spoilt by another blaze of publicity and so I made off across country behind the Tor."

"And you got bogged," said Richardson, "and had to get your clothing cleaned by the night-porter at your hotel in Plymouth, and your suit—the one made by Langridge & West of Sackville Street—was spoilt."

"Good Lord! That suit was made before I left England, but of course I hadn't used it much. You seem to have been following the footsteps of the great practitioner whose name was Holmes, and this"—he pointed to Jago, writing busily at the table—"must be Dr. Watson in the flesh."

"Reddy let you know that Instone was dead?"

"Yes; I sent him down to find out, and that was the report he brought back, so of course I had to lie low. I gave Reddy my address to write to me in Paris, and he sent me blood-curdling stories about how sleuths from Scotland Yard were on my track. Now what are you going to do with me?"

Chapter Twenty-Three

"THAT DOESN'T rest with me, sir," said Richardson. "I must ask you to stay in this room while I consult higher authority."

Richardson went first to Superintendent Witchard.

"That man about whom you issued a memorandum to the Port Officers yesterday has come over voluntarily. I met him at Dover this morning and he has just made and signed a full confession, so the notice to the Port Officers may be withdrawn."

The Superintendent made a pencil note on his blotting-pad.

"And now, sir, I should like to get a ruling from Mr. Morden."

"Have you sent the man over to Cannon Row?"

"No, sir; I haven't charged him. He is simply waiting in the Chief Inspector's room with Sergeant Jago. Can you take me now to see Mr. Morden?"

Witchard rose rather ungraciously. "Come along then, I'll take you in now."

To Morden Richardson recounted what had been done since he last saw him. "My difficulty is, sir, what is to be done with this man, Willis? He is a man of means and can provide for his defence. He admits that he struck the blow from which the man Instone, alias Dearborn, really died, but he pleads that the blow was struck in self-defence, and there are two eye-witnesses of the incident to prove this."

"He means to plead justifiable homicide?" asked Morden.

"Yes, sir, if he is charged at all, and that would be a matter for the Director of Public Prosecutions."

"Who hasn't yet seen the papers? If you charge him at all he will have to come before the court. If you don't charge him within the twenty-four hours he may bolt."

"I don't think he will do that, sir."

"What is your view, Mr. Witchard?" asked Morden.

"I think the whole inquiry has been a waste of money, sir. It ought to have been possible to drop the case at an earlier stage than this, if it was to be dropped at all. The written statements of these two eye-witnesses of yours were enough to prove that the blow was struck in self-defence."

"Pardon me, sir. Everything turned upon who was the aggressor. The man who stopped the car may have had the intention to commit an assault upon its occupant and then, of course, he would be liable to indictment as the occupant of the car might have used the starting-handle to defend himself. But we know now that the occupant was the aggressor; he jumped out of the car and struck the first blow. He was armed with a weapon of metal, the other man had nothing but a wooden walking-stick. I submit that the act of leaving the car showed Instone to have been the aggressor, quite apart from the evidence of the two eye-witnesses. Until I could get to the bottom of the case there was no real proof which was the aggressor."

"I see your argument, Mr. Richardson," said Morden; "but the question before us is whether this man Willis is to be arrested and charged or what is to be done with him. If we charge him the magistrate will admit him to bail and then the newspaper racket will begin."

"I don't think he'll bolt, sir, if we let him go home. What he wants is to have the case disposed of one way or the other."

"What do you say, Mr. Witchard?" said Morden.

"It's always safer to follow the legal road, sir; then there can be no agitation against the police."

"I agree," said Morden, "but this case is exceptional, and if Mr. Richardson feels sure that he can trust him, I'm inclined to let the man go home on the usual understanding that he comes here when he is sent for."

"Very good, sir."

"In the meantime," said Morden, "you ought to take those papers over personally to the Director of Public Prosecutions, explain the circumstances orally to him, leave the papers with him and take his instructions. For the time being, as you know, you become his servant."

"Very good, sir; in the meantime I should like with your permission to straighten out all this money business between the various witnesses by dealing with them personally."

"What money business?"

"Well, sir, I have a five-hundred-pound note belonging to Lady Penmore which was found among Instone's property and proved that he had stolen it; then there is the question of the money left by will to Instone's widow; it was stolen money and she wishes to surrender it to its rightful owners without legal proceedings."

"Strange woman," observed Morden under his breath.

"We are not concerned with the money invested in this gold mine by Miss Straight. Willis will see to all that himself."

"It seems to be a pretty complicated case, but as you know all the details you'd better do all the clearing up. It won't cost much in travelling expenses, will it?"

"No, sir; only one journey down to Bath."

"Good; then we'll consider that settled, subject to the views of the Director."

Richardson returned to his room and explained the situation to Willis.

"You mean that I'm free to go home?" he asked in astonishment.

"Yes, subject to your parole to present yourself whenever called upon."

"I'm very much obliged to you, Mr. Richardson. You can count upon me remembering for the future that when one has a grievance against one's fellow man it is always best to come first to the police. If you don't mind touching the hand of a homicide I should like to shake hands with you. Goodbye."

Having ascertained that the report for the Director of Public Prosecutions could not possibly be ready before the evening of the next day, Richardson looked up the trains to Bath for the next morning, and decided to use that evening for coming to an understanding with Mrs. Dearborn, as she still called herself.

"I was wondering when you were coming to see me, Mr. Richardson. I want you to tell me frankly all about the money my late husband left to me and how he got it."

Very gently Richardson told her everything. He could see by her expression how she was fitting the information into the chain of facts already known to her.

"Then none of this money is mine," she said, "if it was all embezzled."

"But Mr. Sutcliffe, to whom it rightfully belongs, wishes you to accept some of it."

"I won't accept more than just enough to keep me until I get work. Perhaps he'll be kind enough to recommend me for some employment."

"I am going to see someone to-morrow morning who may make the kind of offer to you that you would accept. I will arrange for the lady to write to you, and you will settle the money business direct with Mr. Sutcliffe."

At twelve o'clock next morning Richardson found himself on the front steps of Lady Penmore's house in Bath. Her welcome was plain-spoken.

"Well, Chief Inspector, who have you been arresting for this murder? Not my poor son, I hope, though he ought to have been put under arrest long ago, just to teach him obedience to the law and to his mother."

"We have found the man who killed Instone, Lady Penmore."

"Then I hope he will be suitably rewarded, for if ever a man wanted killing it was that scoundrel Instone."

"I have your five-hundred-pound note in my pocket, Lady Penmore."

"Do you expect me to fall on your neck and kiss you before you give it back to me?"

"No," laughed Richardson, "but I do ask for one favour." He told her about Instone's widow and her need for paid employment.

"Do you mean that there's a woman in England who's been left twenty-five thousand pounds and wants to give it up without going to law about it? Haven't you sent for the usual two doctors to certify her?"

"No; she's very far from being certifiable. She wants to do the right thing."

"Strange woman; I should like to see her. Is she fond of dogs and cats and things?"

"I believe she is."

"Then she'll fill an aching void. I've always wanted a kennel-maid who will keep my pets from telescoping."

"Telescoping, Lady Penmore?"

"Yes; the canary fits into the cat and the cat fits into the dog, and there's no peace under this roof. I've always wanted a kennel-maid, but I never knew how to find one. Send her down to me."

Richardson rose and began to thank her.

"Oh, that's how it's done. A little pretty talk and then one walks out of the house five hundred pounds to the good."

Richardson pulled the envelope out of his pocket. "If I give you this, Lady Penmore, there is one proviso, that if it's wanted for the trial you will be ready to produce it in evidence."

"Shall I be called as a witness?" she asked with glistening eyes. "I should love to tell a British judge and jury what I really think of them."

On his return to London Richardson found his report ready for the decision of the Director of Public Prosecutions. The Assistant Director, a criminal barrister of great experience, listened patiently to his story and read all the supporting documents.

"I can give you a decision off-hand," he said. "It is not a case in which we should have any chance of success and it would be a waste of public money. You shall have a decision in writing to that effect when I've explained the details to the Director."

"And I can tell Frank Willis that there will be no prosecution?"

"Yes."

By six o'clock Richardson found himself at the Bromley garage. There he imparted the good news.

"I suppose if I'd stood my trial," said Willis, "it would have made Sutcliffe's innocence clear to the world."

"In a sense, sir, it would, but many people would have said that he had no right to allow himself to be robbed of his clients' money."

"You're quite right," said Sutcliffe. "It was my duty to protect their money and I allowed that rascal to steal it. We've had a lively morning with the widow," he added. "She wouldn't hear of retaining a penny of that money beyond her expenses for two weeks."

"But after we'd gone down on our hands and knees to her, she agreed to accept some shares in our mine," said Willis.

As he finished speaking the telephone bell rang. Sutcliffe went to it. He came back grinning. "So you haven't been idle, Mr. Richardson. The widow has rung up to say that Lady Penmore has offered her a job as kennel-maid on quite good terms and she's accepted it."

"I think, sir, that she's the sort of woman who'll be much happier like that than if she were heiress to twenty-five thousand pounds."

Richardson took leave of his new friends with the regret that he always felt when he brought a case successfully to its final conclusion.

THE END

Printed in Great Britain
by Amazon